Temporary

Hilary Leichter

Temporary

faber

First published in the UK in 2021
by Faber & Faber Ltd
Bloomsbury House
74–77 Great Russell Street
London WC1B 3DA

First published in the United States in 2020
by Emily Books, an imprint of Coffee House Press
www.coffeehousepress.org

Typeset by Faber & Faber Ltd
Printed in the UK by CPI Group (UK) Ltd, Croydon, CR0 4YY

A CIP record for this book
is available from the British Library

ISBN 978-0-571-36386-5

2 4 6 8 10 9 7 5 3 1

for Mom

It seemed to me that if she could remain transient here, she would not have to leave.

MARILYNNE ROBINSON, *HOUSEKEEPING*

Onboarding

There was the assassin. There was the child. There was the marketing and the fundraising and also the development. There was the keeper of the donor list. There was the shredder of the master list. There was the washer, and there was the dryer, and there was she who dispensed the dryer sheets. She donned them like veils, then dropped them in the machine. There was the folder of socks. There was the dropper of bombs. There was the knocker of doors. How many people live in your home, and would you like to support our cause? Will you buy some citrus fruit? Would you care for some literature? There was the house with the doors that opened and closed. There were solutions that needed managing. There was the shepherd of pamphlets. There was the checker of facts and, later, the checker of spells. There was the learning on the job, and the lying on the job. There was late for work, and there was early. There was even right on time. The box of stamps and the corkboard calendar and the pink book of message sheets to tell you what happened exactly, specifically, in detail, While You Were Out.

City Work

I have a shorthand kind of career. Short tasks, short stays, short skirts. My temp agency is an uptown pleasure dome of powder-scented women in sensible shoes. As is customary, I place my employment in their manicured hands. With trusty carpal alchemy they knead my resume into a series of paychecks that constitute a life. The calls come on Mondays and Fridays, flanking each week with ephemeral placements. Like clockwork, like something sturdier than time, the agency allots my existence. After I prove reliably discreet and efficient, I am sent to various priority clients. Personal assistant jobs. Jobs assisting with personal things. "There is nothing more personal than doing your job," something I read on a granola bar wrapper on my way to work. It's a sentiment strong enough on which to hang my heart and purpose.

My boyfriends call these positions A Great Opportunity, but they're company men. They carry comedic mugs to their offices and leave them on their desks overnight, little pools of sludge staining the ceramic bottoms. In the coffee grounds I divine their fortunes: my boyfriends will go gray at these same desks while purchasing cubicle-sized funeral plots.

I worry about those poor, abandoned mugs. How sad they must feel, how lonely, left to sit in their own filth. I worry about living the life of an unwashed vessel. The mold that fissures the leftover coffee, floating like a lily pad on forgotten dregs.

"But what's your dream job?" my earnest boyfriend asks, his chin cupped in his hands.

"It's hard to explain," I say.

"Try!"

I consider my deepest wish. There are days I think I've achieved it, and then it's gone, like a sneeze that gets swallowed. I've heard that at the first sign of permanence, the heart rate can increase, and blood can rise in the cheeks. I've read the brochures, the pamphlets. Some temporaries swear it's that shiver, that elevated pulse, that prickly sweat, the biology of how you know it's happening to you. I worry I'll miss it, simply overlook the symptoms of my own permanence arriving. *The steadiness*, they call it.

"When you know, you just *know*," the lucky temps say. "You can't rush these things."

Some temps never go steady, and they die before digging into the footholds of life.

"My dream job is a job that stays," I tell my boyfriend. "It might not happen tomorrow, or overnight. One morning, I'll wake up and be just like you."

"Baby, you can be whatever you wanna be!" He smooths my hair with both hands, and it poufs back out again in the wake of his touch.

My earnest boyfriend does not live with me, he who plucks the spiders from my rug and tucks them onto window ledges. None of my boyfriends live with me, but some of their weekend sweaters do—pilling, furry creatures in my closet of corporate attire. I occasionally return the wrong sweater to the wrong man, but they don't notice. We aren't anything long-term, they know. They have their nights of the week, their weeks of the month, a chain of open sweater arms spreading toward Sunday like woolen paper dolls.

I introduced them to my mother but only once, following the prescribed rules of the temporary life. She reviewed their pictures in advance, the photos unfurling from my wallet in a slim accordion that grazed her kitchen floor.

"This one," she said. "Nice eyes."

"My culinary boyfriend."

"Your tummy will always be full. Good girl. And him?"

"My tallest boyfriend."

"Hmm. Doesn't look very tall."

"Well, the camera cut him off a bit."

"Hmm."

"This one's my favorite," I said, shuffling the selfies and headshots. She squinted to assess his particular grin. "Do you approve?"

"What do I look like, a matchmaker?" she asked, tossing the pictures on the table, disappointed in this gesture I'd made at constancy.

In my mother's kitchen, the mugs were clean and dry and stacked in a far cabinet. Her dresses were starched and pressed, and her lips were colored with something called a stain. Even when she wasn't feeling well, she wore her favorite earrings.

"Be reasonable," I can still hear her say, "and tell me about your jobs."

Farren is my primary contact at the agency. Her face is fresh and lip glossed, a properly moisturized beacon of confidence and self-care. Her nails are always painted with a sparkly glitter polish, fingertips flashing from below her neutral sleeves like hidden constellations peeking through the clouds. So these are the hands reaching down from the sky, I think, shuffling forms and contracts to guarantee me some honest employment.

During our initial interview, she hoisted herself atop her desk and seated me in her comfortable chair. The arrangement felt as strange and unsettled as if she'd scaled the ceiling and harnessed me to a system of ropes. I wondered if it was a test and struggled to maintain an alert position.

"How's this?" she asked, shoving a pile of papers to the side with a flourish to make room for her legs.

"Wow, Farren, this is just great." The lumbar support immediately put me at ease, into a trance, or both.

Did I fall asleep? Maybe.

What happened next, I'm not entirely certain. Perhaps this was the specific moment of ergonomic telepathy, the agency's chance to divine my pure internal mechanism. The secret gear, the hidden nut or bolt at my core that revealed the truest rhythm of my potential for labor. And then: a shiver, a swift unease, like a swiveling chair that tips back a notch too far. Maybe this is what the steadiness feels like, I thought, my mind careening forward down a narrow, hopeful lane. I checked my pulse. I listened for a tune or a bell or another oblique sign that I had been granted permanence.

But no—provisional employment rushed back through my veins. Everything was familiar and fleeting again.

"You OK?" Farren asked. She handed me a form and touched my elbow with a cold, outstretched tip of shimmering nail. Just the nail, not the finger. I couldn't tell if it was meant to soothe or scratch.

"I'm fine. Thanks, Farren."

"Good! Because I wouldn't want you to miss out on this *dream* placement!"

I didn't want to miss out either. I don't. I'm filling out forms, always. I'm shaking hands. I'm gainfully employed, again and again and again. The surest path to permanence is to do my placements, and to do them well.

Everyone knows Farren's priority clients are top of the heap. Heads of state and heads of house, leaders of industry, leaders of followers.

I worked my way up like anyone else, starting with the bottom-barrel business, those city-living jobs that make a city pretty.

I shined the shoes of important showmen and watched them tap and hoof themselves all the way through Grand Central. They taught me a few moves on the sly.

I washed the windows on skyscrapers that truly scraped the skies, those cloud-raking tines of weather vanes, satellites, rods of steel like stilettos. I could squeegee and dance my way down the sides of the buildings, shimmy shimmy shake, falling for what felt like miles. "From roof to Duluth," my fellow washers would say.

"From the sky to a slice of pie" was the usual response, and then we'd all go grab some coffee and apple crumb, or cheese-cake, or whatever was on special.

Next I tried my hand at directing traffic. The stop and the start of it all. Then I tried my feet at pounding the pavement. But literally, with a jackhammer. And filling in for the mail-man. Filling in for the mural artist on Tenth Street. Filling in for that woman who hails a taxi every afternoon at that huge intersection, you know the one. She hails that cab with such gusto, and the tourists love it to death. But I don't ever hop in the cab. I just hail it.

Finally Farren sends me to fill in for the Chairman of the Board at the very, very major corporation, Major Corp.

I sign documents I don't understand, sit in on conference calls, stack memos and stamp the dates, fiduciary and filibuster and finance and finesse and fill the office walls with art selected from a list of hip emerging painters, and finish each assignment before anything can be explained in full. Everyone has a parcel of work they don't want to do themselves, and what can I say? I'm a purveyor of finished parcels.

As Chairman of the Board, I wear a fashionable dotted scarf with my suit, knotted around my collar so it resembles a tie. "Details count for something," my mother used to say, "but not for everything."

"And what of today's vote?" my assistant asks. The boardroom is lively, and all are in attendance. I take my place at the head of the table.

"Well," says a shareholder, "might I encourage a show of hands?"

"No, no," says a more significant shareholder. "An anonymous vote or no vote at all."

"Spoken like someone who hasn't been to a meeting in a year," mutters the first shareholder.

"I have various commitments!"

"I propose a new kind of vote," says an entirely insignificant shareholder, "in which we vote the way we think our grandmothers would've voted, contrast this against the votes our unborn grandchildren might make, then, using a system of charts and graphs, concede to the hypotenuse of the two hypotheticals, in the name of our forbearers and our descendants."

"*That* shareholder is entirely insignificant," my assistant whispers to me.

"Can I ask," I say, clearing my throat, "what are we voting on, exactly?"

"We are voting on the frequency and content of future votes!" everyone chants in unison.

"Or," says a man at the far end of the table, "you know, maybe we could just put a pin in it?"

At the suggestion of pins, there are audible sighs of relief. "Yes, yes, yes," the room agrees. From their briefcases emerge a proliferation of tacks, which they stick into the leather flesh of the briefing books. And the meeting is done.

The Major Corp office building is one of great proportions and minor distinctions. The coffee is hot and the soda is warm and the snack pantry is plentiful, boasting a bumper crop of bananas and candies and granola bars. There is a microwave that smells of popcorn. Cigarette breaks are long and recommended, so I learn to smoke my mandatory smoke, knowing that someday, for another job, I'll probably need to unlearn the habit, knock the bitter twist from my lip. I put that knowledge in the bottom of my bag like a receipt.

Smoking my very third cigarette ever, I see a woman standing near the exit. She weeps, loudly, and I consider that in one
of my morning meetings, I probably put a pin in her employment. Or worse. I pass her my dotted scarf to dry her tears
and enter the role of comforting stranger, which isn't a paid
placement but one I feel fit to cover nonetheless.

"I've worked here for twenty-four years," she says with a
large sob.

"I've worked here for twenty-four hours!" I say, squeezing
her shoulder. She laughs and receives the comfort with real class.
It's a real good deed to let someone else comfort you, because
the comfort goes both ways. I'm grateful to her for letting me
perform this function. I give her shoulder one more squeeze,
then a third miscalculated squeeze, then a fourth and truly un-
advisable squeeze. She has magnificent arms. What brand of
idiot would fire someone with such magnificent arms?

"Um, OK," she says. She smiles over her potentially injured
shoulder as she walks away. She probably thinks I'm nobody,
and I am.

I stay after hours on my last day at Major Corp. I like to
loosen the boundaries of my employment and remain longer
than I'm needed. I can feel my necessity slipping away with
every extra minute; it's a rich, complicated sort of sensation,
like napping, or dying.

And how I love an office building in the evening! I can
pee in the bathroom anonymously. I can clean dirty mugs,
construct rubber band booby traps, paper clip trapezoids.
A motion sensor controls the overhead lights, so when my

colleagues have gone home for the night, I retreat to the dim, postfluorescent glow of my temporary corner office. There is nothing lonelier than lights extinguishing themselves at the end of a long day, no one left to do them the simple kindness of snuffing out.

On my final snack pantry excursion, between the towers of Twizzlers, I find I'm not alone. A man sits at the rear of the snug enclosure, shelling pistachios one-handed.

"Are you quite done?" he asks. "With your work?"

"Nearly," I say to the real Chairman of the Board. I recognize him from his portrait in the lobby but not from the portrait in his office, which does him no justice. He's a string bean in a suit, with a full head of white hair and a pocket square in his coat. I maybe recognize him from somewhere else too. After all, he's a prominent figure, both numerically and physically.

"Why are you hiding?" I ask.

"I'm not hiding, I'm dying." He shells a nut and eats it, then eats each half of the shell. "Now that you're done replacing me," he asks, "are you available for a new job? I have an unusual request."

I direct him to the agency, to Farren, but they've already been in touch. Life moves faster than protocol. It's in this way that a small box arrives on my stoop. In the box is an urn, and in the urn is the man, and the man is dust.

"You are meant to carry him with you," Farren explains, "so he can be about town. See, he was a man about town, and now he still is."

"When does the assignment end?" I ask.

"When does anything end in this infinite world?" asks Farren. I can hear her starry fingertips tapping on her desk.

It's a messy task to transfer the Chairman into the necklace charm. With the help of my handy boyfriend, I construct a miniature paper funnel and pour the remains in an unsteady stream.

A repurposed gift from my handy boyfriend, the necklace trinket once held a tiny bubble of his favorite bourbon. I remember his chapped face on the cold night he presented it from his pocket like a rabbit from a hat, so resourceful and kind, his eyes welling with satisfaction. Jewelry, a sign of attachment, I've been told. Also pets, plants.

"I *made* this for you!" he said, a sliver of expectation gilding his voice.

He undid the clasp with thick, gloved fingers, the kind of minor feat that usually charms my socks off.

He expected me to wear the necklace always. The expectation puddled in his every pore. He was ever lying in wait for congratulations on this one nice thing he did this one time. Luckily, since I didn't see my handy boyfriend more than once a month, I could construct a fable in which I wore the necklace every day. In this story I wore the necklace noon and night, and I didn't by any means take it off each time we parted ways.

It's pretty. It looks antique, like something with history.

It isn't that I don't love the necklace. I just don't love giving anyone the wrong idea, or even the right idea. I don't want to give any ideas at all. I certainly didn't want to hurt my handy boyfriend.

Now, funneling ashes on my apartment floor, he shows no real sign of distaste for the task, no indication of anger. But a quiet, burgeoning grimace tempts the corners of his smile, as if to say, Well, this isn't what I expected.

After several spills, a heap of ashes on the rug, a consultation with a vacuum, and a visit from the lint brush, we succeed in transplanting a sample of the Chairman and securing his rightful place on my person. I lift my hair from the back of my neck in preparation for the chain. I lift my shirt in preparation for my boyfriend.

Later, while my handy boyfriend snoozes on the couch, I tuck the rest of the Chairman's remains back in the box. Back in the rear of my closet, back into the square foot where the closet extends beyond the door like a burrow in the wall, a snack pantry, a catacomb, a tomb, beyond my corporate chain-link purses, studded clutches, striped shells, and slitted skirts, furry sweaters standing guard.

What about a funeral? What about his family? I wonder.

The first payment from the Chairman's estate arrives in my bank account the next day. The necklace starts to burn the following week.

"So this is how the other half lives!" the Chairman says. He's standing on my couch, touching the ceiling, until he jumps down and sits on the floor.

"How?" I ask. "How are you here?"

"I'm a man about town," he says, like this is all very obvious.

I look at my necklace, then look at him. "Do you grant wishes?" I ask.

"What do I look like, a genie?" he says, vanishing into thin air.

The boyfriends grow used to these antics. Me, suddenly staring at an empty chair. Me, talking to myself at the dinner table.

"I see the Chairman has decided to join us tonight!" my agnostic boyfriend says, cracking his knuckles and dying for a debate about death.

"Is he, like, really tall?" my tallest boyfriend asks on occasion. "Like taller than me?"

"Close," I say.

"What have you told him about me?" my favorite boyfriend asks, and I lie. The truth is, I haven't told him anything at all.

"When are you going to take me about town?" the Chairman sometimes complains. "I'm a man about it and we never go anywhere. We never do anything!"

I put on some sneakers and take him for a run in the park, but the dogs distract him. He tries, and fails, to pet every single one.

When the Chairman leaves for the day, I put my sneakers in the hall. The shoes I'm hired to fill are constantly switching in size.

A certain woman who needed her closet of shoes arranged kept me in her employ for years.

"Yes, there's the old woman who lived in a shoe," Farren explained, "but these are the old shoes who live with a woman."

"I think I can manage that."

"That's the spirit!" Farren said. "If you do well with this, I can assign you some of our other Mother Goose listings."

I almost laughed, but Farren wasn't kidding. I know a temp who worked a couple shifts doing curds and whey. Farren tried to send her back for a three-month placement.

"No whey," the temp said. "Take your tuffet and stuff it."

In confidence, I learned that she had a better offer from an agency out west, working with wheat and chaff. Still, with that kind of attitude, I'm sure she docked herself a few years on the road to permanence.

The woman who lived with her old shoes had a large uptown apartment with ceilings higher than I'd ever seen. She unearthed from the back of her storage space a marvelous bronze shoe rack, shaped like a nautilus shell. It is the same shape found in the angle of flight the hawk employs to devour its prey. The hawk, with her eyes spread out on the sides of her head, dives down to earth in a heavy spiral so she can always keep her target in view.

"See, they fit like so," the woman said, and she took a bright orange loafer and fed it into a slot. "You can arrange them by heel height, or by color," she explained. "Your choice!"

She delegated this bit of freedom with the implied philanthropy of an angel investor.

"What about arranging them by frequency of use?" I asked.

"Oh, I never wear these shoes," she laughed. "That's a different closet for a different day."

I never saw that other closet, not once.

The woman who lived with her shoes didn't live with another living soul. I permitted her a range of unsavory behaviors as concession to this fact. She liked to change the parameters of my job such that each task's completion was just a later task for undoing. A box moved to would later move fro. The groceries carried upstairs were left to rot, molt, and travel back down the stairs and into the bin. At first I considered this a kindness, a way of manufacturing work when there was none. I now understand it to be a sort of game, the kind of constant undoing that leaves no actual accomplishment, that makes a person question her very existence.

You might think I took out my frustrations on her shoes, but that would be a misdirected rage, and my aim is true. I cradled her shoes with the utmost care, warding off scuffs and blemishes, wiping the dust with a damp towel and dry cloth. Waxing, polishing, smoothing. I admit to performing a tap dance with my hands stuffed in a particular set of patent leather kitten heels, a holdover from my days shining shoes at Grand Central Station. But I didn't dare stretch a single pair with my own large feet. When my employer left for lunch, I touched a pink suede pump to my cheek, and it was as soft as a pet. It smelled new and old at the same time.

My grandmother had a musty closet of sturdy wedges, not nearly as satisfying as these of the woman who lived with her shoes.

On weekends, I was filling in for the mannequins at a local department store to earn some extra cash. The window designer arranged our limbs in fanciful tableaus.

"Rest your arm on this cupcake," he'd say, lifting my elbow so it sat on a life-sized dollop of frosting and cherry. "Make me believe that this sponsored bakery product is providing you solace," he'd say, adjusting my palms toward the sky in supplication. "Give me dessert eyes."

For the holidays, we mannequins stood silent as snow in a diorama punctuated by glitter and tinsel and light.

My mall rat boyfriend often came to visit me at the food court for dinner. Pretzels, takeaway dumplings. He had a car, and sometimes he would drive me home from work. I liked the feel of the cracked upholstery on his passenger seat, the kind of damage that suggests aggressive comfort. So much luxurious comfort I'd start snoring now and then, seat belted to protect from collapsing into the dashboard.

"I like it when you stay in costume after work," he said once.

I was wearing a lion-tamer getup, heavy on the tassels. "Give me lion eyes," the window designer had said, "like you've tamed the lion and now you *are* the lion, but also, not."

One evening, on my way to meet my mall rat boyfriend, I made a detour through Women's Fashion, and there she was. My employer, the woman who lived with her shoes. She sat knee-deep in sneakers, slip-ons, stilettos, mules, boxes and sizes and styles aplenty strewn around her tiny form. If I'd left a moment sooner, I might not have seen her walk away in a pair of crisp moccasins, down the aisle, and straight out the exit without paying for her purchase, leaving her own old oxfords stacked neatly near a cushioned bench.

This is why, later that week, I felt comfortable swiping a particularly lush pair from her closet. A size too small for me, but still, a shoe for a shoe. I couldn't bear to watch them waste away in disuse a moment longer.

Now, at the bar with the tallest boyfriend, I wear the pair in question: high zipperless boots that slide on and off only with great difficulty. The labor is always worth the result; they transform my limbs into calligraphy. On the phone with Farren, I click my heels against the stool. She has a new job lined up, just for me.

"What are the particulars?" I ask. My tallest boyfriend has commandeered the bartender's attention on account of his height, and he secures for me a vodka soda.

"That depends," Farren says with a hint of ellipsis. "Do you have experience with, or training in, seasickness?"

"Seasickness," I repeat. My tallest boyfriend raises an eyebrow, which somehow makes him taller.

"It's not on your resume, so I had to check." Farren says. "Answer honestly."

When Farren says to answer honestly, it really means to please be more comfortable lying. I try to feel comfort with this skill every day, practicing mostly on myself.

Seasickness, I think, but not out loud. I touch the Chairman of the Board where he hangs around my neck.

"Remember," Farren says. "Sometimes you have to leave home to earn permanence. There are opportunities for diligence and efficiency in many realms. This is your chance to find the steadiness. The world is infinite, and the work is, like, endless, am I right?"

Within the hour, I'm shuttled away from the bar in a black van and placed on a large boat. The pirate captain hands me time cards and a confidentiality agreement, and so the whole affair starts to feel official. We spit on our palms to seal the deal. The boyfriends come to the dock to say good-bye, and I can see them running from separate points toward the water, waving in the distance, little specks with arms in the air, my men.

The gods created the First Temporary so they could take a break. "Let there be some spare time," they said, "and cover for us, won't you? Here are all our passwords and credentials. Here is the keycard, and here is a doohickey to clip the keycard to your purse. See? Oh, sorry, here is a purse. Go on, fill it to the brim! Fill it a little more. Yes, it's supposed to be heavy. Here is your contract, and here is our copier, and here is the shared binder for all known manner of things."

The First Temporary fell from the husk of a meteor and glowed with no particular ambition. The gods had to pin her down so she would not float away, so distracted was this new kind of soul, so subject to drift. To be fair, they had not yet invented gravity. This was back when toads without occupation soared straight up to the clouds, back when employment was the only kind of honest weight you could apply to a life.

The Temporary spent her first day of work reading the shared binder for all known manner of things. She familiarized herself with each section, each document. Birds, bees, mitochondria. She noted how overfull the binder was even then, even when the world was mostly long stretches of empty surface. What looked blank was actually cluttered with microscopic tendencies toward life. There were infinite itemizations to complete. If the world was already so stuffed, would there ever be room for the First Temporary? The word placement *meant something very different back then. It was not a job or a gainful assignment of employment. It was simply a place for each thing, a place to belong. The First Temporary assigned placements for trees and sandy shores, for fossils and tassels. She wondered about her placement, its unsteadiness.*

"Can I stay? Permanently?" she asked, and the gods just laughed and went to lunch.

At the end of the day, when the gods went to their god homes, the First Temporary thought, What should I do now? The office had a smell that happened only at night. "That's the smell of innovation," the gods had explained. She found one corner of the office that didn't smell so much and sat there for a while. It wasn't really an office, not the way most people today would picture an office. It was a collection of matter and inertia that suggested the sensation of work.

She activated her keycard and swiped herself into existence.

Water Work

I'm filling in for someone named Darla on the nautical voyage of an unmarked vessel. "Ahoy!" I say. I'm met with some ahoys in kind. I'm also met with some harrumphs and howdys and plain old hellos. I understand. Like any new company, they're still working out the kinks. Still oiling the gears of their mission statement, garrisoning their prospectus. The prow of the ship has no mermaid, and the flag that flies has no logo.

"Not yet, but soon!" the pirate captain says. "We're considering proposals."

My new mates carry weaponry in varying degrees: a dagger here, a pistol there, a cannon on occasion. This is a relief. The worst kinds of offices are the ones where no one can tell who's in charge. My new crew was once a company of internet pirates, but they rebranded. Delete a few syllables and lo, you have a new profession.

"There are only a few kinds of jobs in the world, it turns out," says the captain, who is the type to pontificate and listicle on subjects varied and profound. "Jobs on land," he continues, "jobs at sea, jobs in the sky, jobs of the mind, and working remotely."

"You mean like working from home?" I ask.

"No," the pirate captain says. "Working remotely is what

we call being dead. Pirate lingo."

"Oh sure! Like Davy Jones's locker?"

"No, no," he says, exasperated. "That's where we keep the office supplies."

"Right. Sorry."

"You'll get the hang of it," he says with a slap on my back. "The world allows for periods of adjustment."

And how grand it is to see that world! Most of the world is water, and so to my mind, I've now encountered the meat of the matter. Yes, my flaneur boyfriend makes his annual pilgrimage to Paris. But has he traveled the shivery narrows at the gut of the Atlantic? Excluding the part where his plane flies over the Atlantic? There's salt in my nose and salt between my toes, and I can't wait to send a postcard from my new, beautiful, briny life. She's really going places, is something my boyfriends are maybe saying about me.

The predicted and dreaded seasickness aggregates somewhere at the back of my tongue. I try to hide it so as not to be caught in a resume fib. I keep a bucket close. When my stomach swings left, I lean starboard. When my stomach swings right, I lean port. In the process, I learn about starboard and port! I try to compensate for the waves roiling in my belly. I hang my head over the side of the ship, and the first mate of human resources finds me swinging there.

"I'm the first mate of human resources," he says. He flips me across his broad shoulders, walks me down into the hull, and carries me to his office. I haven't been carried in such a very long time.

"Sit here," he says, placing me on his sofa, "until you're fit to function."

The human resources cabin is mostly bare. A large poster on the wall features a cat with a peg leg paw. "There is no Purr in Pirate!" reads the caption.

"Are you OK?" the first mate asks.

I nod, but the nodding is too much like bobbing.

"Great. Let's assess the situation. Did the food make you ill? Or was it something one of your superiors said?"

"No, neither," I say.

"Do you have a particularly sensitive gag reflex?"

"I don't think so."

"OK. Are you pregnant?"

"What?"

"If a woman is sick at work, she is probably pregnant. Those are the rules!"

"I'm not."

"Great, great. I'm just covering all the bases. Because your resume here says you can, quote, totally handle seasickness."

A lump rises in the back of my throat. I swallow it down, but swallowing is like swaying. I lean back into the cushions, but it's really more like falling. The perspiration on my upper lip desperately needs attention.

"My bucket?" I ask, and he nudges it closer to me. "Thanks."

"Not *your* bucket," he says with a laugh. "Company property."

"Right," I say.

"By which I mean to say, treat it as such."

"Right."

"By which I mean to say, you probably wouldn't want to relieve yourself on company property. Right?"

"Right."

"Now." He sits down in a swiveling chair across from me. The rotations of the wheels are disastrous. "About your alleged seasickness."

"Oh no, it's not that," I try to explain, my face glistening with sweat. "Not seasickness."

"No?"

"No," I gag, and my head goes into the bucket. With a single swoop, he pulls my hair back from my face, and he doesn't stop there. He produces a band from a drawer filled with such accoutrements and braids the length of my tangled mane. He's done this before, I can tell, the yanking and the coaxing, the application of product. He pulls the braid forward over one shoulder and pins it around the crown of my head in a sort of, well, crown.

"This is a fresh, hot look," he says while I wipe my mouth.

I do feel fresh, and hot. Then he puts his index finger at the base of my skull and gives my newly exposed spine a long, silent stroke. At first I think he's picking up stray wisps at the nape of my neck, pinning them out of view. But no, it's a different ritual, one I don't recognize.

"In human resources," he says, "we provide resources to make sure you're as human as possible. I'll leave you with some pamphlets about company property and resume accuracy. Here," he says, and he puts the pamphlets in my lap.

Somehow the literature on my legs soothes my stomach.

"Thanks."

"For the seasickness," he says, "there is a cure. It's easy. Just think about how much you want the job."

"I want the job very much!" I manage to say, wiping my mouth.

"That's great. Because you know what happens to land legs that don't acclimate?" He points to the peg leg kitten.

I give him a thumbs-up, which is all he needs. He smiles.

"Remember that I helped you! Remember, I'm your trusty HR mate. Helping is what mates do," the first mate of human resources says. He extinguishes the cabin light with two damp fingers, closes the door, and lets me get some sleep.

Come morning, I've been terrified into excellent health. A note on the door reads, "A clean bucket is an acceptable bucket, and an acceptable bucket is the only kind of bucket worth filling."

I file the daily logs and keep the desk materials neat and orderly. I swab the deck and stack the clean company buckets. I find a corner of clutter that hasn't been dealt with properly, and I deal with it. I study *The Pirate Book of Burdens*, *The Pirate Book of Crimes*, and *The Young Pirate's Book of Crafts*. The job blooms before me at its own pace: These things can't be rushed.

They pay me decently on this boat, just as Farren promised, though I suppose I can't judge the fairness of my salary, having no experience with boats. Then again, I do recall a skinny canoe from childhood, settling on the side of a grassy lake.

One particular paycheck comes in the form of three red stones, clear at their centers, taped inside a windowed envelope.

The man who handles the payroll has long, twisty hair and a dimple in his chin. He wanders the ship at night, repeating conversations from earlier in the day. He reminds me of my caffeinated boyfriend, the one I date for suspense. Sometimes he perches on a post, nose to the sky, flapping his arms ever so slightly.

"He's filling in for our parrot, Maurice," the executive assistant explains.

I see this parrot man every evening from afar, after I finish organizing the daily logs. I'm excited to meet another temporary.

When our paths finally cross, he stops me with his hand, or wing. He puts his other hand-wing on the small of my back and walks me to a quiet corner. He breaks character, the entirety of his face softening and hardening in unexpected ways. I think I notice a rapid growth of stubble where there is none. He's brand new. He tells me that soon I will walk the plank.

"They'll throw you overboard, just wait," he says calmly. He's not like my caffeinated boyfriend at all. His hand, still pressed against my back, doesn't shake. His hand, as steady as a wall.

"Sorry?"

"Just wait. You'll walk the plank."

"I don't understand," I say.

"I'm just saying," he says, then he walks away, as if saying something out loud is ever a minor thing. He rearranges his body to once again replicate Maurice the parrot.

I don't pay much attention to him. No one does. Every office has a long-haired man who doesn't trim his sideburns, who tells his coworkers things they don't want to hear, who does a passable impression of a bird. If he gets under my skin, I can report him to the first mate of human resources. Or I can go to my desk, the miniature porthole where I watch the waves and feel at ease. The view isn't life changing, but it's nice. I've seldom had a window at my workspace, and certainly none with an ocean lookout.

Most everyone else is friendly in an affirmative, nodding sort of way. There's a woman in a patchwork skirt who makes conversation with me every morning, waiting in line for grub.

She says, "Good morning, Darla!"

I say, "Good morning to you!"

She looks supremely disappointed shoveling hash browns onto her plate, knowing I'm not Darla, that I have no desire to be Darla, that I'm not even in character as Darla, that I'm only humoring her. It takes an aggressive empathy to accurately replace a person. A person is a tangle of nerves and veins and relationships, and one must untangle the tangle like repairing a knotted necklace and wrap oneself at the center of the mess.

I concentrate over my scrambled eggs. I try to feel Darla's absence as it relates to every other person, using an ancient meditation technique that temporaries sometimes find helpful. It's not a standard brand of meditation. In fact, the average employee might call it "staring." The woman in the patchwork skirt sits alone but stares back at me with quiet ferocity. I sense Darla is someone both loved and feared, and I try to adjust my temperament to properly fill her boots. I slap a lot of backs and laugh a lot of laughs, and other times I walk the deck with stern and hollow eyes. A little of this, a little of that.

"Not bad," the captain says, encountering me on one of my jaunts. "Not bad at all."

"Thanks," I say, but then I wonder, Would Darla give thanks?

Under a sunset sky and over a dinner of fish chowder, my coworkers explain what Darla would never do.

"Never would Darla do to others as they would do to her," says the pirate captain.

"She would do them one better!" says his executive assistant, who's always stealing punch lines for himself. The captain rolls his eyes.

"Never would Darla steal a lady's pudding," says the woman in the patchwork skirt, "especially if the pudding was clearly labeled with the name Pearl."

"Never would Darla brew herself some coffee," says the executive assistant, "then retrieve the coffee and leave the old grounds sitting there for no purpose other than to prevent someone else from easily brewing a fresh pot of coffee. Never would Darla not brew a fresh pot after she had enjoyed her own coffee, and this is the most important bit, write this down: Never would she claim credit for the new, fresh coffee she brewed, for a fresh pot of coffee without credit is like a love note in your locker—it's just magic, and if you take credit, you might as well not have made any coffee in the first place, at all, not ever, never! It's like, What, you want a medal for making coffee? Know what I mean?"

"Would Darla ever drink some ale?" I ask.

"Darla would," says the woman in the patchwork skirt, whose name is Pearl, and she passes me the canteen with a firm thrust of approval. I'm getting the hang of this, I think.

"Never would she ask for overtime," says the pirate captain.

"Hear, hear!"

"Not Darla!"

"And never would she ask for severance," adds the pirate captain.

"For she's the one who does the severing!" exclaims the executive assistant, laughing and laughing. At this point the captain lifts the executive assistant in the air by his collar and tosses him overboard. We sit for a moment in silence.

"Darla," says the pirate captain's wife, using her spoon as a baton, "would never not dance," and she conducts us across the deck, where we dance until dawn. The moon hangs high, and the boat careens from side to side against a blue horizon. We sway together and apart. We do the customary moves, the shuffles and kicks and awkward thrusts. The parrot man plays guitar, and Pearl plays drums.

"Conga!" the captain cries, and conga we must.

We situate ourselves to sleep under the fading stars, and I think of Farren's glittered fingers twinkling in the early morning sky. The wind blows over our bodies like a cool cotton sheet.

"Never would Darla not do something asked of her," whispers the first mate of human resources. His head is perpendicular to my body.

"Compliance is a great skill!" I reply.

"Never," he says, his hand flat on my thigh, "would she say no. Because then she wouldn't be Darla." He uses all his various human resources to roll on top of me. "Darla does this all the time."

"Really?" I ask.

"Sure," he says, pressing down. "Sort of."

So it is understood now that the crew requires something different from me than they require of Darla. It isn't unheard of to provide assistance for needs not normally associated with a given position. I behave in accordance with the first mate of human resources' insisted understanding of Darla. He isn't the first man to miscalculate what a woman would or wouldn't do, and with his hands under my skirt under the sails under the sky, no one hears a thing, least of all Darla.

Late that night, or early that morning, I feel my necklace burn against my chest. I wander to the edge of the plank, where I find the Chairman of the Board sitting and eating his pistachios.

"So, is the pirate life the life for you?" he asks.

"Yo-ho, I don't know."

"Make an effort, kid! You're barely trying."

"I am trying. I'm putting my best self forward."

"Oh yes? Which self is that?" he asks.

I think of my many available selves, coagulated and discrete, compromising themselves for one another.

"Where's the ambition?" he cries. "Where's the cutthroat spirit?"

"That's not really my style," I say, toeing the edge of the plank.

"Let me tell you something about style," he says. "Style was the name of my first poodle. I once bought an island called Style, and pronounced it *stee-lay*, just because I could. I basically invented style."

I look off to the horizon in the hope of seeing the Chairman's island. When I look back, he's gone.

Most everyone on deck is still asleep. The first mate of human resources is snuggled against himself in a satisfied pile of person. The executive assistant climbs the rope ladder back aboard the boat, his clothes sopping wet.

"Hi," he says, embarrassed. Then he goes downstairs to change.

I brew him the best pot of coffee he's ever had in his life, and I clean the filter, and then I brew another, and another, and we don't exchange a single word about it.

On my lunch break, I use the main office below deck to call the boyfriends. Specifically, I call the funny insurance salesman. He always has a joke or two, a story to spin for his girl.

When he answers his phone, he's at my apartment. He let himself in with a spare key to pick up an old sweater, and he ran into two of the other boyfriends. They're all sitting on the sofa watching the big game. Would I mind if they continued to watch games on the sofa, and maybe also the Oscars and the People's Choice Awards, and perhaps some other television events? They have so much in common, my boyfriends, so much to say to each other, it turns out.

"Of course I don't mind," I say. "I'm a good sport!"

"Did you say you're good at sports?" my insurance salesman asks. It's loud in my apartment. Someone has scored something, and someone has reacted.

"Yes, that's right," I say.

"She's good at everything!" I hear in the background, and I recognize the voice of my life coach boyfriend. I haven't seen him in a while, but he assures me that time multiplied by distance equals the square root of affection and long-term achievement. He has an infographic illustrating this very point, and it hangs on the wall above his bed.

It's truly great to hear them shout hello at the receiver. The receiver catches my voice when I feel as if my voice might break. "Static," I say. It's great to hear me shout hello, too, the boyfriends agree.

"Since you're already there," I say, "would you mind giving my jade a drink?"

"Not at all!" I hear the running of my tap, the walking across my room, the nourishment of my plant.

"And bringing in the mail?" I ask.

"It's the least we can do," my tallest boyfriend says.

I've received a total of four catalogs, three takeout menus, and two once-in-a-lifetime urgent money-back zero-interest limited offers. I've also received a letter from the lady who lives with her shoes.

"A former employer," I explain. "Tell me what it says?"

My life coach boyfriend clears his throat and recites the handwritten diatribe against me, my knees, my feet, my toes— the way the middle toe, in the name of all that is blasphemous, tucks under another toe, the way the pinky toe is like the crushed, stemless strawberry at the bottom of the basket that nobody wants to eat—and yes, yes, yes, does she really have to say it? She knows I stole her boots, her babies, and why, and how, and what did she do to deserve such insolence? And when can she expect the boots to be returned? And yes, she knows that old saying about walking a mile in someone else's shoes as a way of better understanding and loving the various people in your life, but if I've treaded so much as a square of tile in her precious kicks, if I've stretched them even an inch with my wide-footed waddle, so help her god, or so help her whatever kind of god a shoe-stealing thief like me even deems a deity, for scuff's sake, she'll teach me a lesson, she'll make me pay.

The television fills the phone with crunchy half noises.

"Are you going to be away for much longer?" asks my bright-eyed insurance salesman, he who specializes in my human worth.

"Probably not," I say, "but business is hard to predict." I like saying *business* this way. As in, my business, not yours.

"We'll take good care of each other while you're gone," he says. "Don't worry a bit."

I cheer at this with a single, stretchy *yay*. But it also makes me feel as hollow as a cave, and the phone cuts out before I can offer anything resembling a real good-bye.

The exact nature of the vessel's work is unclear, but I rarely have insight into my employers' overarching projects. Pearl explains, sitting with me in the crow's nest, that we're looking for investors and will steal them if we have to. Soon we'll go hunting for venture capital.

"The captain calls it adventure capital," she says, her feet dangling over the deck below like two birds circling each other in a miniature chase. "Treasure," she whispers.

"Is it dangerous?"

"Of course," she says, "but in the wrong hands, so are staplers."

Pearl is a skilled negotiator, each mediation a literal notch in her belt. She's carried off the grandest thefts and convinced the victims they were winners. *Let's find a solution that suits us both*, she says, while her mates pillage and rummage and plunder. Her trademark tactic. She brags that if she wanted, she could convince the captain to promote her to captain instead. She could convince the sky to thunder. She could convince a fish to fly.

"You mean like a flying fish?" I ask.

"No, like a gull. Like a goddamn gull."

It bothers her that none of her colleagues wear an eye

patch. "It would make my job so much easier," she says, and she tries to talk me into donning a vintage variety sewn of brown leather, featuring a delicate embroidered skull.

"It would really add to our overall visual brand," she says.

"I'm good, thanks."

"But it would look so great with your hair!"

"Really, no thanks. I don't need it."

"If *needing* it is the problem, I could make it so you need the patch forever," Pearl offers. Would she scoop out my eye for the sake of appearances? I guess people do much worse for the sake of appearances.

"What I meant was," I say, "wouldn't it better suit the first mate of human resources?"

"That guy?" she asks. But maybe she sees my face tighten, and she doesn't press or push the subject. "OK," she says. "I like a challenge," and she puts the patch back in her pocket.

The man with the long, twisty hair comes to perform his parrot duties in the crow's nest, and so we climb down and leave him to his feathered work. When I glance back in his direction, he's watching me with his true face, the face that looks harder and softer at the same time.

On our day off, Pearl and I circle the deck in the ovoid patterns that fuel good conversation. "Good walk, good talk," my gym rat boyfriend used to say, and even my mall rat boyfriend couldn't deny the benefits of a long department store stroll.

Pearl walks on the periphery and I march next to her. We both like popcorn. We both like peeling sunburns. We're both bad at first impressions. I open my wallet and let the long ribbon of boyfriends fall to the ground. Pearl examines their faces with respect and interest.

"Nice chin," she says. Nice this, nice that.

Over brandy, Pearl patiently shows me how to tie a halyard knot, a bowline, a half hitch. My fingers are raw from the roughness of the rope.

"Here," she says, massaging them with a cool cream. It feels good to hold hands, even if the holding isn't the purpose, just a symptom of a separate action.

"Now untie," she says, and there's something so persuasive about her sweet, rich voice. I dig my fingers back into the knots and detangle.

"You're a natural," she says, indicating my attempt at a sheepshank. "Darla would be so impressed."

"I'm not natural at anything," I say, rubbing my hands. "I mean, you were born for this," I say, and a shard of jealousy lodges somewhere in my side.

Pearl frowns. "How can you say what I was born for or against?" she asks.

She has a point. What do I know about anything? Pearl sits in her chair and runs her hands over her face, like putting on a mask, or taking one off. This is the way someone looks when history lodges in their throat, and I know I'm now meant to hear a story, specifically, hers.

"I nearly wasn't born at all," Pearl explains. "And by no means was I born for this, or for any particular vocation. I was born to replace other births that didn't go as well. I was born as my parents' final attempt. I was born very small and very early. That's why for the rest of my life I've always tried to be right on time."

"Punctuality is a great skill," I say.

"True," she agrees. "It's good to know where you're meant to be, and when. I know that if I follow this rule, from time to time I'll find myself filling the empty space left by someone who came too late or arrived too soon."

"You could call that an advantage," I say.

"You could. There are advantages to filling in. Here I'm just filling in for a woman named Pearl who never came back. That was two years ago. Now I'm permanent Pearl."

"Well, you're the only Pearl I've ever known, so you're just plain Pearl to me."

"Thanks, that's sure nice of you to say. But I'll never plainly be Pearl. I'll never be anyone until I feel the steadiness. All I can do is try to convince you that I'm successfully inhabiting the current target of my approximations."

"I understand."

"It's like in *The Pirate Book of Burdens*," Pearl says. "The burden of being at sea."

Pearl teaches me all the knots, knots I've never encountered before. There's a knot that resembles a fish, but it's called the bird. A special series of knots that when tied just right reveal a sort of written code. She shows me a knot called the evolution, named for the way it gradually tightens over time. If you leave the evolution alone for a month, it grows tighter than a gnarled root. There are evolution knots at the bottom of the ocean, buried in sunken ships, perhaps the tightest tangles you can find on the surface of the earth.

It's getting late, the sky dumping its golden glow all over the deck. When the moon is crescent, the pirate crew does movie night. Team building. A projector fastened to steady hooks, the sails are suddenly a screen. Men and women in black and white projected four stories high, billowing and expanding with the wind. The pirate captain loves the classics, and he smiles his face off.

"This summer, we'll do a retrospective," he says, "of films I enjoy."

If the actors weren't so elegant, they could just as easily be giants standing on water, stomping us to smithereens with their high artifice and witty quips and speedy barbs, the kind of quick dialogue that lets you know everyone is ultimately in love but not in love until the last minute. The heart is a fast, thumping creature, like a metronome for repartee. In the movie, everyone talks without breathing just in case they die before they get a chance to articulate their feelings. The final frame is always a tight embrace, a resuscitation. It wouldn't take much to get me into the crow's nest tonight, to rest in the arms of these characters, these people pretending at other people.

Pearl sits beside me and offers handfuls of her popcorn. I remember with fondness and pity the sad kernels stuck to the sides of the Major Corp microwave. It's not homesickness that I'm feeling. Jobsickness. Seasickness. Pearl laughs when I laugh, and I know the movie will now be a joke between us, the plot as real as a story that happened to us and only us, in our life, together.

We walk back to our sleeping quarters. I quicken my pace past human resources but not enough for Pearl to notice. Outside my door, she grabs my cracked, brittle hand, now coated with the grainy, buttery residue from my first fun night in many nights.

"Darla is my best friend," she says.

"I know," I say.

"If she doesn't come back, maybe . . . you can be Darla."

Permanent Darla, I think. Would that be steady enough?

"Maybe you can be my best friend," Pearl says, and I fill up like something empty, something fierce and starving. Of course, of course, of course I take her eye patch. I even wear it. She adjusts it on my face and lets her hand linger there, resting against my cheek. We go to my bunk and practice more, this time a different kind of knot.

Temporaries measure their pregnancies in hours, not weeks. We're employed at an hourly rate, and we gestate in the same manner. My mother was pregnant with me for 6,450 hours, most of them billable hours spent at work, filing, tabulating, eating noodles at her desk, then lying on the couch with her feet propped up on a pillow, taking walks around the city with soothing music playing in her ears, sewing elastic into the waists of her pants, going to work, eating noodles, tabulating, sewing onesies, hiding the pregnancy under loose sweaters for fear of dismissal, filling in at work, filling out in the middle, eating noodles, tabulating, swollen feet propped up on a pillow, loose sweaters stretching, walks around the city, music, more noodles.

"Be careful, or you'll end up *unemployed*," my grandmother told her. My mother had never heard her say that word out loud before.

"Not in front of the baby!" my mother said, putting a hand on her belly.

"Be cautious, or you'll wind up working for a witch," my grandmother said.

This wasn't just a turn of phrase. There is nothing worse than working for a witch, nothing more shameful, the very last measure of hope for the unemployable temp, and in hour 4,016 of her pregnancy, that's exactly where my mother landed.

My mother wasn't particularly forthcoming with the details.

"Mostly paperwork," she'd say when I'd ask her about it, my fingers stretched over my eyes. I was expecting strange and wonderful supernatural terrors.

"Oh sure, some cauldron scrubbing. Double-checking spells, fact-checking potions. The occasional graveyard roundup, the occasional subterranean ritual."

My jaw would go slack, and my mother would straighten her blouse.

"Mostly errands," she'd say.

"What about goblins?" I would ask. "What about brooms?"

But my mother would just shrug, eat her noodles.

In truth, while she was working for the witch, there were consequences to consider. She was concerned the job might leave some mysterious residue on her pregnancy, on me. When she traveled home in the evenings, with each stretch of pavement, she'd count the hours to make sure I wasn't too early, or too late, but still arriving very much right on time, perfectly on schedule.

Around hour 6,430, the witch drove my mother to the hospital.

"She drove? Why didn't she just fly?" I asked.

My mother laughed. "You try flying with a final-hour pregnancy strapped on your back!" she said.

Birthdays aren't a serious affair for temporaries. Usually, one simply adopts the birthday of the employee one has replaced. No cake, no streamers, no banners, unless those banners say, "Happy Birthday, Karen," and I'm replacing Karen on her birthday. And yet, every year I wake up at the exact hour and minute on the day I was born, and I can remember that night, emerging and landing in my mother's arms, passing over to my grandmother's lap in the seat by the window, and finally to the small and dainty hands of the witch.

I never mentioned it to her, but my mother was onto something, worrying about that residue. I know it was the witch who engineered this yearly birthday memory, her thumb tapping my brow, forcing me to acknowledge something about myself, even when my self is tucked away, deep in the pockets of another person.

I think about this, sleeping next to Pearl on the evening of my birth, in the guise of Darla, my head on the pillow and my palms tucked under my cheek.

A scream startles me awake first, then the splashing, then the linking of the boats.

"Pearl," I say, shaking her with both hands. "Pearl, what's happening?"

She snores, rolls over, and splays her body across the bed with the stretch of a starfish.

I rise from the bunks and pull myself up the stairs, slowly so as not to disturb. The scene: a smaller boat next to ours, full of passengers. The passengers are lifted onto our deck one by one, then carried below. I remember the first mate of human resources carrying my seasick body. Now he carries a different young woman in the same fashion. Adventure capital.

I duck under a tarp and watch the capture through my unpatched eye. Pearl's patch, I learn, allows for me to shift from above deck to below, to consider various levels of light and dark without losing my vision or experiencing glare. From under the tarp, my view might be obstructed, but I can see what I need to see.

The capture isn't violent in the traditional sense. No one is outwardly harmed, but there's harm everywhere. There are weapons at the ready.

"Let's make this easy on everyone!" I hear the executive

assistant say, his arms open in supplication, each of his hands occupied with a dagger.

I see the captain's face, so close to mine that I could reach out and touch it. And maybe it's the moonlight or the wind, or the tiny bites of frosty water spraying his skeleton crew, but my affable boss from hours earlier is nowhere to be found in this strange, square visage. The corners of his eyes are vicious, and his mouth is turned down and out and small. I see, for a sharp, pinched moment, his teeth.

The remaining hostages are secured in the dungeon, and I creep back to my quarters alone, expecting to find Pearl under the blanket, her skin cold and clammy. The bed is empty. I will now practice barricading my door at night. All nocturnal journeys will occur within the confines of my room. I will climb the bunks until my muscles turn fantastic, until I can defend myself against whatever treachery arises.

In the morning, I expect a company meeting. All hands, as it goes. But nothing happens. One day slips by, then another. I slip knots and unslip them. I keep the desk materials clean and orderly. No one says a word about our acquisition. Our merger? Our acquisition. Normally, on land, I would consult human resources, but here I am at sea. The invaded ship is nowhere to be found. At the bottom of the ocean is my guess, which is as good a guess as any.

I follow Pearl, hoping for a talk.

"Do you have a minute to chat?" I shout after her.

"Sorry, I'm completely underwater with work!"

She quickens her pace but says over her shoulder,

mid-sprint, "Not literally underwater!" She smiles, so I know we're still best friends.

Everyone smiles. Everyone smiles over dinner, over breakfast, the smiles lingering long past the meals, and onward into the evening for the passing of ale. Everyone is happy, and now I fear I'm imagining the things I saw at night. Was any of it real, or is this one of the Chairman's new tricks? I hesitate to share my knowledge for fear my spying and snooping make me unforgivably less of a Darla. I hold on to my new knowledge like a life preserver, and I wonder if I'm sinking anyone else by keeping this secret.

Another day goes by, and another.

Payroll arrives on my desk: the man-parrot gives me a small box, which I tear open in his presence. Nestled in tissue paper I see a studded, sparkling brooch in the shape of a nautilus shell.

"Appropriate, no?" he asks. "For our life at sea."

"Look at my bracelet!" Pearl says, popping her head in my office and holding out her wrist. "Real pearls!"

There are silk scarves and necklaces and gold belt buckles to go around. There are coins for some and bills for others. We're worth what we're worth. I think of the captives below, pants falling down, wrists and necks newly bare, pockets empty, and I hold the blinding brooch in my palm. I put it away with my rubies, my paychecks, my new possessions. Maybe these jewels will be appraised for next to nothing, I think. Maybe they're of no value, not even the sentimental kind. Maybe my brooch doesn't belong to the captives in the truest sense of belonging, but who am I to know what it means to belong—to a person, to a place, to a time? Which is to say, maybe a captive simply stole the brooch from some other captive, who stole it from another captive, who again stole it from another, from another, provenance indeterminate. If I can separate myself from the crime by several degrees, the crime feels less criminal.

I try to feel comfort with lying every day, practicing mostly on myself.

A whole week has passed when the captain raps his knuckles on my door.

"Yes?"

"Today you will do inventory," he says with a smile. "Follow me."

I gather myself and trail the pirate captain to the dungeon, where we see the prisoners sitting, playing chess, taking naps. They look well rested and fed, and no one is bruised or bloodied. I'm thankful that, for a dungeon, it doesn't really smell. Everyone looks surprisingly OK. But then again, so do I.

"Create a file for each of them," he says, handing me a legal pad and an inky pen. "The usual details."

I pull a chair up to the edge of the dungeon bars. I run my hands over my face in the manner of removing a mask, or putting one on, in preparation for their stories. Their ages, twenty-four to fifty-eight. Their heights, their weights. The sizes of their shirts, extra small through extra large. Blue eyes versus brown versus hazel, differences in color of hair, in length, in texture. Where do you see yourself in five years? When do you fall asleep at night? When do you wake up in the morning? What is your biggest flaw, and don't say you're a perfectionist. How many teeth do you have in your head? Where were you going, out on the open sea?

"We were on a work retreat!" one prisoner says.

"I rented a glass-bottomed boat. For team building," a woman says, and I assume she's the boss. "I'm the boss," she whispers, curling down to the dungeon floor in a gesture that says, *This is all my fault.*

"We could see all the fish. Every single fish."

"I saw a shark!" someone says.

"No you didn't. You did not see a shark. That wasn't a shark."

"Joe was just using the glass bottom to look at people's reflected bottoms."

"Joe was not doing that!" says Joe.

"There were iridescent jellyfish as far as you could see."

"We were all looking down," the boss says, "when *you* captured us."

"Let's get back to inventory," I say, uncertain of how to proceed.

Data. Education. Religious beliefs. Relevant experiences. Previous abductions. Future aspirations. Life skills. Leverage. Their children, their pets, sons, daughters, twins, older brothers, older sisters. Their spouses, some present, some absent, some absent in the final sense of the word. Their first loves. Their last meals.

"Most recent meals, you mean!" a prisoner yells for clarification.

"No last meals today, right?" Joe asks, stepping forward with a squeak.

"I'm not sure," I say, and I'm telling the truth.

Their bad deeds. Their good deeds. An old lady carrying groceries. A dog stuck in a tree.

"Isn't it usually a cat stuck in a tree?" I ask.

"That's what makes my deed especially good!" says the woman who rescued the dog in the tree.

Any detail that might save their lives. Any detail that might explain their lives. Their vacations and date nights and nightmares and bad years and boring choices. The marrow of all their mistakes. Their levels of inexperience. Their jobs, their jobs, their jobs, their jobs.

Then a small voice from the back: "My job is that I used to work on this ship."

A woman in a patchwork skirt steps forward. All the air is sucked forward and out and away.

"My name," she says after a pause, "is Pearl."

"Of course, she's lying," says my Pearl.

The entire crew is gathered in the dungeon to see her, this woman who claims to be the original Pearl.

"Why would I lie about something like this?" original Pearl asks. She isn't panicked, nor is she calm. Her voice is like a rubber band stretched taut. The stretching involves some invisible, silent control. She's about ten years younger than my Pearl, and they look nothing alike. There shouldn't be a debate at all, in theory. This Pearl is tall and lanky, straight lines and long limbs. My Pearl is shorter than me, curvy in her patchwork skirt, her wrinkled blouse.

"Look at her skirt," my Pearl says, putting a hand on my shoulder. "A dead rip-off of mine."

"I think it might be her," the captain says, peering at the prisoner Pearl's face, "but I really couldn't say. She was so very far below my pay grade. I'm not remunerated for looking down, right?" His eyes widen with a bit of recognition, and he turns to our Pearl for reassurance, or for an explanation.

"It can't be her, not logically," my Pearl says. "Because I'm the original Pearl."

The pirate crew whispers and stares, murmurs with great uncertainty. I watch in disbelief as Pearl convinces every person in the room that there was no Pearl before her, and no Pearl who could possibly replace her.

"Look back through all your memories of our ship," she says. "Brand new, stolen straight from the dock. Look back through every single moment we've spent together. Look into my eyes. Me, managing receipts. Me, leading plunder initiatives. Me, having affairs with you and doing lunches with you and covering for you and ratting on you and trimming your beards, cutting your hair, waxing your chests. Me, smashing a bottle of champagne against the side of the ship as a blessing. Me, scooping a net of four hundred bluefish from the salty depths."

"But that was me! That was all me!" the prisoner Pearl says, her sentences getting sharper, anxious. "I told you everything when you replaced me. I told you everything."

"Me, writing the procedures for dealing with liars and traitors and pirate deserters."

"I wrote those procedures," the original Pearl says with despair, or is she the original Pearl after all? I start to wonder. It's all very convincing. It's all very confusing. No one is ever exactly who they claim to be, but some people are closer than others. Who's to say the prisoner Pearl is still even Pearl after all her time away? Who's to say I'll still be myself a year from now? Twenty years on, someone might be more my current self than I ever could have been.

Now the prisoner Pearl is crying. "My procedures," she stutters.

"If you wrote the procedures," our Pearl says, "then you'll

63

know the standard protocol. You'll know it's about time we commenced the severing!"

The pirate crew cheers, and my best friend Pearl stands on a stool.

"But here's the most important bit," she explains, her voice softening. "Let's say this is the true Pearl, here in her cell. Let's say she isn't the lying, traitorous captive we know her to be. Let's say she's half as pretty as me, or even two-thirds as smoking hot. Even if this unimpressive patchwork sack was indeed your original hire, dear captain, sir. Even if this garbage skirt human is who she claims to be, though we know she isn't. I challenge anyone here to name a name for me that isn't Pearl, and I'll switch with her bony rump in an instant, throw myself in chains. I challenge you all: If I'm not Pearl, then tell me, who am I? What is my name?"

The pirate crew is raucous with excitement, for when they see my friend, the only name they see is Pearl. They cheer again.

"Do we, the most ferocious pirates on Earth, judge things by how they start? Does it matter who stirs the pot if someone else serves the stew? Does it matter who mends the dress if someone else wears it? It's the woman who finishes the job who gets the job done!"

"Sever her! Sever the Pearl imposter!" someone shouts.

"And we all know," says my best friend Pearl, "who does the severing."

Every man and woman stands back, until I'm left at the center of a circle. Pearl hands me a knife larger than any I've ever seen, even the gourmet knives in my culinary boyfriend's precious butchering set.

"Oh, that's *definitely* Darla's job," the captain says, his arms crossed over his chest. "Without a doubt."

"Any limb will do," Pearl says, and the crew leaves me to my work.

An hour or so after dawn, my best friend Pearl notices that the alleged-original Pearl is no longer in the dungeon. She's no longer anywhere to be found.

"Well?" she asks me, a glint of something in her eye that makes my torso lean away. She is surrounded by a throng of pirates, hands on their daggers and swords. They have come to find me at my desk.

"It's done," I say, keeping my face cool and even.

"And?" Pearl continues. "Where is she?"

"She's no longer with us," I explain. "She's no longer your concern."

"Did you sever a limb?" Pearl is getting frustrated. The captain peeks around the corner, then leans on the doorjamb to listen.

"No, not a limb," I say. "I severed her head."

The first mate of human resources delivers an audible gasp. Someone else passes out. The pirate captain's wife covers her mouth. The parrot man narrows his eyes.

Pearl smiles. "I don't believe you," she says. I have anticipated her disbelief.

"In *The Pirate Book of Burdens*," I offer, launching my voice loud and clear, "what is the most important burden of all?"

"The burden of proof!" the executive assistant yelps, unable to contain himself.

"It's true," the captain says. "We pirates, as a people, are wholly concerned with proof."

"Yes," I say. "And here is my proof."

I present to Pearl the sword covered in blood. Now her jaw drops. Now she's impressed.

"I severed her head and heard her spine crunch and turned her into fish food. No one lies about my friend Pearl, at least not to my face."

My mates applaud.

"Now her face is gone for good," I add, with a grotesque flourish. "She'll work remotely the rest of her days."

Pearl holds the bloody sword for a moment, for a knife that commits a deed such as mine is no longer a knife but only a sword. She looks at me long and hard and surprised, and I feel as if it's been a long time since Pearl was surprised by anyone, any thought, anything. And then she embraces me. A resuscitation. Everyone cheers. They lift me and carry me out across the deck, whooping and hollering. For she's a jolly good fellow. Which nobody can deny.

"There's the trail of blood, leading to the plank!" someone shouts.

"You can see where she dragged the Pearl who isn't Pearl to her watery grave!"

"So much proof, like, *everywhere*!"

"No offense to Darla," I hear the executive assistant say, "but I think this lady's even better!"

We dance and kick and shuffle. I lean against my dancing partners to hold myself up. The pirate captain grabs me by the waist and pulls me close during a ballad.

"We should talk about your future," he whispers in my ear. "So much potential."

"So much potential indeed!" the pirate captain's wife agrees, coming around and swaying me into a pirate sandwich. Then she pats me on the head, and her husband pushes me over to a group that dances me into their arms. I wince as they throw me in the air, catch me, throw me, catch me with their open, welcoming hands.

"You're our favorite!" they say, except for the first mate of human resources, who knows he can never say anything to me ever again.

My head spins with joy. I return to my cabin late that night, after drinking and twirling and drinking and leaping. I'm full to the brim. I unwrap the wound on my thigh that bloodied the sword. All the dancing has reopened the cut where I sliced my skin, and blood oozes down into my stolen boots. Maybe now I'll be permanent. Maybe this is the start of the steadiness. In some careers, you draw blood to make an eternal bond. In others, you draw blood to fake an eternal bond. I hide the drenched gauze behind my pillow and wonder if the escape went as planned, if the prisoner Pearl has made it safely ashore. More than being good at my jobs, I'm good at procrastinating. I'll find any way to put off a task. Indefinitely.

And is this what it means to belong? Still drunk on the feelings from above deck, I tuck myself under the covers. It's a question I've asked myself before, half-awake, on occasion, with my hands propped behind my head: Once after meeting a new friend. Again in the sweaty nook of my favorite boyfriend's elbow, the discomfort of his sleeping position somehow only further proof of acceptance and inclusion. Is this what it feels like? I ask no one in particular. Even the seclusion of my bunk seems somehow possessive and true, not lonely, not isolated, just privacy as proof of permanence.

At some point in the middle of the night, I hear an incredible crash, then screams, then cries of despair. I climb upstairs after redressing my self-inflicted injury. At first I think, Another capture? But the tears turn to laughter, and the higher I climb, the better I can hear sweet chimes between the sobs. The tears are tears of joy. A woman stands on the prow of the ship in silhouette with the confidence of someone who holds a perennial soul, who can leave as often as she wants, who can always come back. It's fitting. Just when I'm feeling the thrill of the open waters, just when I'm finding my place in the crew, just when I'm learning to tie all the types of rope knots on my grub breaks, just when the captain asks me to consider my future, Pearl climbs the prow to tackle this silhouetted woman in a series of hugs. Darla has returned.

I'm done filling in for Darla, who was visiting her grandparents in Florida.

"I'll never retire," she says. She rips the cap off a bottle of cider with her teeth. "Too much free time."

She's brought souvenirs for her coworkers, which is a pretty classy thing to do. A snow globe for the captain. A severed finger for Pearl. A box of saltwater taffy for the people she doesn't know as well. I help myself to a piece, impressed again with the company ethos and very sorry to leave.

My assignment ends the next day, and I prepare my possessions. I receive a final payment: a single, heavy coin. I'm thrown overboard sometime midafternoon, my belongings taped to my chest. Darla thanks me for covering for me as I'm walking the plank.

"From what I hear, you're a real gem," she says, and she throws a life preserver down to express her gratitude. It floats far off and away on a wave. "It's not personal," she says. "It's just a job."

"There is nothing more personal than doing your job," I say.

They're throwing the man with long hair overboard too. Maurice—the actual parrot—has returned in his full-feathered glory, chirping and singing and circling the sails.

"I told you so" is something the man doesn't say, but he looks at me in a way that basically says everything else.

I look back at the captain, at Pearl, at my new friends. Pearl turns away, and the captain gives me a big thumbs-up. This isn't the good-bye I anticipated, but then again, I didn't anticipate good-bye at all. I'm ashamed to admit it.

"Good-bye, Pearl!" I shout, but she's busy talking to her one true best friend. I see now how little like Darla I am, how little like me she is, how we are not at all like each other. She gallops around the deck with the confidence of a horse, her hair pulled into a bun, tiny curls slipping from underneath. The tiny curls look just like mine. I can always find a curl like this, and despite the situation, despite the fate before me, I smile. When I'm gone, a tendril will remain.

We stand on the plank, the former Maurice and I. I'm scared to jump, but there are swords at our backs, so I simply loosen my limbs and fall. He grabs me by the hips as we crash into the ocean, and he holds me against his belly for the descent. Salt water comes up, around, and into my ears, and I can't help but respect the man for his clairvoyance. I never seem to see things coming before they've arrived. You'll walk the plank, he said all those weeks ago. Now the plank is nothing but a shadow in a mirror world we're leaving. It looks like an extended limb, and then—vanished.

We sink deeper, and the world opens wide beneath us. The world is deep and fills itself. I start to fill with water. Seasickness. There's no purr in pirate. I open my eyes and think I see his lips moving, bubbles darting around his nose. "Swim," he mouths. "Swim, swim like it's your job!" His long hair flowers and branches out around his face, and I'm filled with the awe of lying under a large tree on a summer day, the leaves rustling with birds and bugs, a plane flying even farther above the tree, a skinny canoe at the edge of a lake where the water mingles with mud and turns to grass, and that is when my eyes close.

First Work

My mother arranged for me my very first job, just as her mother did for her.

"We work," she said, "but then we leave."

She unfolded the family tree of the temporary lives recorded before ours. My aunt with her stack of resumes. My grandmother with her dainty paper coffee cup. My great-grandmother behind a desk, and on the desk, a nameplate with someone else's name. "Filling in!" she had written on the back of the photograph, in legible, steady script.

"I'm just filling in. You're just filling in," my mother explained. "See?"

She didn't have to explain. I already knew it in my bones, in my knees, in the way you understand things about yourself even before you hear them spoken aloud. I knew I, too, would always find myself somewhere new, someone new, for the rest of my life, like my ancestors, like theirs, like theirs, like theirs. The top of my head measured just above the side of my mother's full blue skirt, where the fabric emptied into a hidden pocket, where unbeknownst to anyone but me, my mother stored a bright set of inky pens.

She drove us for three hours, deep into the suburbs. We stopped along the way for sandwiches, and she said, "Why don't you order for the both of us? I trust you."

I ordered burgers instead, and she applauded my initiative.

"Nice improvisation," she smiled, squeezing ketchup from a packet. We ate at a picnic table under a stately oak until the juice from the burgers soaked the buns, until the birds came to claim our soggy fries. The lake nearby was full of children in canoes, running their fingers through the water, wanting and not wanting to capsize, in equal measure. When I finished my food, I stretched out on the grass and looked up at the light that filtered through the branches of the tree until my mother's face encroached on the view, her head hovering above me like some newly built nest.

"Time to go." She smiled, and we piled back into the car.

We sang along with the radio. Something about the seasons, something about eternal love, and then several songs with lengthy metaphors. She opened her window, then closed it, her short dark hair nicely whipped with wind. I pulled a single leaf from a single strand.

"Thanks, kid," she said in a voice that felt too kind, too sweet, settling a score that hadn't yet been unsettled.

I dozed off with my head tilted all the way forward, as if sleep were a somersault I couldn't complete. When I woke, my mother had pulled over to the side of the road to check her directions.

"What's wrong?" I asked.

"I think we're lost," she said, but I knew that she knew where she was going. She didn't have the frantic flutter of confusion in her eyes. Her finger traced the map with an absent sort of attitude, and she looked straight through the paper to something just beyond the visible world. She was making a decision.

For a long moment, like a dimple in the day, I thought she might turn around and take me back to our living room, our kitchen. The particles of dust hung in midair over the dashboard, and the rearview mirror was filled with homeward potential. Then the moment broke, the engine kicked, and she merged into traffic. Our car continued along its intended route.

When we arrived at my new job, she left me with a leatherbound planner. "To fill your days," she said in the customary fashion, "until none are left."

My mother had no other children, and she adjusted her hosiery as she walked away.

The job was in a lovely little house with a lovely little door. There were more doors inside the house, seven doors precisely, in total. My job was to open the doors, then close them, every forty minutes, every day, all day long, until otherwise notified. The instructions were laminated and taped to the inside of a kitchen cupboard, which, being a cupboard and not strictly a door, I never had to open or close again if I didn't choose to do so.

My favorite door was blue and small. For a child, perhaps, or a pet. The door was at the far end of the house, and it was difficult to see what was on the other side. It only ever opened halfway, but it was important to make sure it was open when specified, even if only a crack, and, later, closed. I had a glorious, shiny wristwatch to keep track of time. But time kept no track of me, and soon my arms and legs shot out and up, and I was grown.

I learned to do everything in forty minutes. Some tasks that were shorter I extended for the sake of clarity and precision. Brushing my teeth, for instance, or combing my hair. A forty-minute sneeze is something I know how to do, and it's not even listed on my resume.

The doors, I imagined, opened to a city somewhere beyond the house, to a knowledge somewhere in the deepest pit of myself. Each squeaky swing closed still felt like an opening, over and over again. Or perhaps the doors kept the house alive, like valves to the atria of the heart, pumping whatever substance the house needed in the right amounts, at the appropriate rate. First the small blue door. Then the master bedroom, the second bedroom, and the third. The bathroom door and the door to the basement and the front door of the lovely little house.

Across the street sat another lovely little house, with a lovely little door surrounded by cream-colored hydrangea. One day, I opened my front door at the scheduled moment, and the front door opened across the street. There, behind the door, was another little girl like me, though neither of us was truly little any longer. She had a glorious, shiny watch like mine, with a tiny face and a skinny gold band.

Her name was Anna, and we met in the center of the road on our quiet street where it seemed no cars ever passed, except for the truck that came to drop off bread and cheese and eggs once a week. We waited at the ends of our driveways, sometimes mine, sometimes hers, and waved at the driver as he drove away.

"Friends?" I asked.

"Neighbors," she said. Then later: "Yes, friends."

We played the customary games. We found ropes and jumped them. We found coins and tossed them. We bet the coins on probable events.

"I bet my house will blow down."

"I bet my house will fly away."

We were two little girls with property, with nothing to our names. We drew straws for keeping track of time. We drew the scotch for which to hop. We drew doodles in our leather-bound planners, but only on the first page and the last. The days have only so much room for frivolity.

Anna's house had a different regimen than mine. Instead of doors, she was instructed to open drawers every hour. Little drawers, big drawers, both deep and shallow.

"Some of the drawers are empty," she explained, "and some are not." She didn't elaborate, and I didn't ask for elaboration.

One morning, we were waiting for the food delivery at the end of Anna's driveway. She sat on the back of the truck, pulled me up beside her, and the truck drove away. We drove past one street and then drove past another.

I realized we were leaving. My face started to burn.

"I promise we'll be back in forty minutes," Anna said.

We drove around the neighborhood and saw many houses

like ours. We saw a shop that sold ice cream, and we hopped off the truck, and we dumped a pile of coins on the counter for two cones, walking back to our street with milky streams trickling down our arms. But the ice cream tasted wrong, and as we approached the end of the block, I dumped the cone on the curb and ran inside my house to close the doors on time.

First the small blue door. Then the master bedroom, the second bedroom, and the third. The bathroom door and the door to the basement and the front door of the lovely little house.

Anna's hair was short, and it curled behind her ears in two tiny wings. In the summer, her bangs stuck to her forehead, like feathers glued to an art project. Her bangs were a source of pride and irritation, always needing the remedy of a clip or a pin. Anna owned a fashionable pin with a tiny rhinestone glued to the bend in the metal.

"I put my pin away in a drawer," Anna explained, her bangs mingling with her eyelashes. "Old habit. Didn't think it was a problem."

"And?"

"Closed the drawer." She mimed the action. "Opened the drawer an hour later, my pin was gone." Her hands went poof, to signal the words *disappeared* and *into thin air.*

We walked down my driveway and up hers, then back again, pretending the street was a moat and the driveways were drawbridges and the houses were castles and we were queens. We bowed to each other, then curtsied and continued our promenade.

"What do your laminated instructions say?" I asked.

"Nothing about this."

"Maybe give it a day or so," I suggested. "Maybe your pin will boomerang back." I did an exaggerated move that involved boomeranging myself away from and back to Anna's side.

She laughed like royalty, or maybe she simpered. "OK," she said. "OK, you're right."

The next day, I saw Anna sitting on the tree stump in her front yard. Her face was a sickly shade of gray.

"I did something bad," she said.

I put an arm around her shoulders.

"I couldn't find my pin, so I took something."

"What did you take?"

"I took something precious," she said, revealing a small set of inky pens identical to my mother's. My eyes widened.

"Where did you get those?" I asked. I said it louder than I intended.

"From the kitchen drawer," Anna said, pulling them away from me. "I thought we could use them to doodle in our planners."

Why were my mother's pens in one of Anna's drawers? I ran back to my house to close the doors again. First the small blue door. Then the master bedroom, the second bedroom, and the third. The bathroom door and the door to the basement and the front door of the lovely little house. I searched every-where for a set of pens of my own, for more of my mother's things. Her stockings folded in a dresser, or her car parked on the street behind my house. I watched Anna's windows through my windows—a figure waltzed upstairs, then back down through the living room. Of course, the figure wasn't my mother, only Anna. Of course, pens can belong to anyone. Of course, there were many pens in the world, I thought, sitting on the floor with my legs crossed. But I was tempted to give my mother a call. Tempted to go home, which of course, for a temp, is not an option.

Later I found Anna at the end of my driveway, her pens arranged neatly on the concrete.

"Can I draw with them?" I asked.

It looked as if all the color had drained from her face, her shirt, her pants, and into the inky pens. She had a translucent quality.

"Here," she said faintly, and her hand barely registered as skin against my fingers. I tried the pens, but they were dry.

"They're dead," I said. Anna grabbed the red pen in a sudden burst of energy and pressed it to the paper so the felt pushed flat. She pulsed it several times, applying force and releasing, like squeezing a heart for a beat, until a small dribble of ink bubbled forth. The droplet sat atop the page in my planner, wet and wide, not sinking in or spreading out as ink is meant to do. When Anna couldn't produce another drop, she pulsed the pen once more, then, with a slow shake of shoulders, she began to cry. I squeezed her shoulder once, twice, three times. I didn't know what to do. After crying for just under sixty minutes, she lifted herself up and away, and floated inside her house to open the drawers. The skies opened, and the rain fell.

First the small blue door. Then the master bedroom, the second bedroom, and the third. The bathroom door and the door to the basement and the front door of the lovely little house.

Anna took more things. She amassed a small pile of stuff. Hairbrushes, photographs, jigsaw puzzle pieces. Lone buttons. Lone items on loan from every single drawer.

"I'm worried," I said. "Should we consult your laminated instructions?"

But Anna didn't respond. She stacked her things in a small suitcase outside, which she had stolen from a deep drawer under the bed. She hid the suitcase under the hydrangea bushes.

"If I take enough from the house, maybe the house will give me back my pin."

The house didn't give back her pin. Anna was sitting in her driveway with me, writing with chalk, and she stood to go inside, to open the drawers on schedule. The house was locked. The back door was locked too. We didn't have keys, and we weren't the ones who locked the doors. Anna ran around the house in a frantic circle. She ran so fast it looked like she was flying.

In a moment of desperation, on behalf of my only friend, I removed my shoe and threw it against a low window. It bounced back, barely leaving a mark. I picked up a rock and tried the harder, jagged solution. The rock bounced back like rubber without a sound. Anna saw my attempts, and before I could grab her, she threw her fist through the window.

"No!" I yelled. But her fist didn't go through. We both knew she had hit it hard enough to break her skin, to break glass. She tried it again and again, and then she used her head. But nothing broke, and nothing shattered, especially not the window.

Anna's jaw hung open. Mine did too. We looked at each other for a moment in silence. Then she adjusted her shirt and dusted off her pants. "I think I've been released from my employment," she said.

"You can stay with me."

She could not stay with me. She tried to enter through the front door of my lovely little house, but her feet stuck to the welcome mat. Whether she couldn't or wouldn't cross, I was never completely sure.

Anna slept in her driveway, no longer concerned with the schedule of drawers. I brought her a slice of bread every morning, and she lined up the slices by the bushes, for the birds. She let her hair go wild and tangled and left her leather planner unattended. I searched my house for contact information, for a phone number or an emergency procedure, but there wasn't a thing available to me.

I once spied the delivery truck parked in Anna's driveway. Then I spied it again, and more times after that. I would wait and watch until the driver emerged from behind the hydrangea bushes. Then, in close pursuit, Anna would stumble through the bushes behind him. Oh Anna, I thought. But the driver is so very old! Then again, watching him, I changed my mind. No, he wasn't very old at all, not much older than us. He might have even been younger, by a minute. And how handsome he was, how his shirt stretched against his chest.

"Anna, here," I said, and I gave her my collection of found coins.

"For what?" she asked.

"For something, or for anything."

"Thanks, really." She smiled and tucked her shoeless feet into the long grass of the lawn.

Early on a Monday morning, Anna took her suitcase and boarded the back of the delivery truck. I watched from the window, too stuck in the midst of opening doors to come downstairs and say good-bye. I pressed my sweaty hand against the glass, and it didn't leave a mark.

First the small blue door. Then the master bedroom, the second bedroom, and the third. The bathroom door and the door to the basement and the front door of the lovely little house.

Without Anna, I was sloppy. I almost missed the schedule by a minute one afternoon, busying myself with daydreams. I felt immaterial and light. I tried to make eggs sunny-side up and broke the yolks in the pan, then scrambled them instead until they formed a thin, papery layer underneath. Sitting with the plate of uneaten eggs, I realized I hadn't been hungry in a very, very long time. The refrigerator, to my horror, was full of bread and eggs and cheese, untouched. I fell asleep at the counter and woke the next day having missed three separate door openings and closings. The smell of old egg filled the kitchen.

What should I do? I panicked. What should I do? What would Anna do? I tried to work backward and consulted my shiny watch. I figured out the doors, at that juncture, should have been closed. I went around as quickly as I could to close them. First the small blue door. Then the master bedroom, the second bedroom, and the third. Everything was going to be fine. The bathroom door and the door to the basement, but the door to the basement was somehow already shut.

I had never been in the house this way, with one of the doors arranged in a different state than the others. Something felt thick and horrible. I had failed. The room conspired and shifted against me, and my cheeks itched, and I could barely stand straight. I reached forward with a long, queasy arm and opened the basement door a crack to correct the inconsistency, then closed it once again. Success.

And there, in the corner of my eye, a shadow darted out of view.

With the doors adjusted, I regained some composure. I could walk again. But the house wasn't lovely anymore, or little. I felt it expand, though I had no proof. I felt the corners darken and deepen, like a drawing smudged with charcoal. My error had upset the house, and the house now upset me. With every opening and closing of the doors, I could see the edges of something leaving just as I arrived, the door a pro-scenium framing a departure, me witnessing the halo of an image exiting the room. First the small blue door. Then the master bedroom, the second bedroom, and the third. The bathroom door and the door to the basement and the front door of the large, haunted house.

I concocted a bowl of oatmeal and left it nestled in my lap, steaming hot, unconsumed. I sat on the floor outside the bathroom door and waited to see who or what was inside. I closed the door on cue, and at the moment it shut, I glimpsed a towel swinging back and forth. My nose filled with the fresh, damp smell of shampooed hair. Then later, to the master bedroom, where upon turning the knob and slowly pulling forward, two entangled figures scattered in opposite directions.

I leaned against the doors to the second bedroom and then the third, hoping to hear a creak or a scratch, a murmur of conversation, a clue. When it was time to pull the doors ajar, the bedrooms smelled messy and busy. A mug of tea and sour milk. A pile of books filled with book smells. The scent of a leather glove, the edge of an arm pumping the air in a cheer, or some other quick, half second of choreography. A single riff of music abandoned and lingering and stale.

Finally the small blue door at the other end of the house, opening only a smidge, revealing the leftover glow of a wet nose and shiny fur, floppy ears and marbled eyes. I ran to open the front door of the house and saw the flash of a completely different street, with cars, with fences, with a different house, not Anna's house, just across the way. Then the flash subsided, and the street as I knew it returned.

I sat on the curb for what felt like hours, but it could only have been forty minutes. It took a few tries to get there, but once I arrived at the thought, it was inescapable, as inescapable as the coins that had cluttered the carpeting. Who dropped those coins for me and Anna to find, and later, who forgot to collect them?

The house was a house for a family, and I was filling in for a ghost.

Years later, I tried to describe the way I came to know my placement had ended. I was sitting on the sofa with my frugal boyfriend, and he had made me a microwaved brownie in a mug. I described the day in question, and he listened, eyes wide. But I knew my words were falling short. I couldn't explain, for instance, how I had one foot in the door, and how one foot wasn't enough. I couldn't admit to having watched the family's edges for so long that I was able to construct a collage of their true nature in my mind. I couldn't, at the time, describe the slice of light that glowed between door and floor, how the promise of this light was actually a slim, dull weapon. I couldn't admit my deepest hope: for the family to finally reveal themselves in full, and for me to join them. But the family wasn't my family. At best, they were my neighbors. Every mother has a set of inky pens hidden in a pocket or a drawer for her daughter. Just because something is familiar does not mean it is mine.

The feeling of ending was the feeling of a new season. My complexion changed, and birthmarks that had gone into permanent hibernation once again rose to the surface. I was suddenly famished. The house unfolded around me like a paper swan laid flat, and the spring air came rushing across my shoulders, and I knew the job was complete. I know this isn't how houses work, but this is how it felt, and it's the only way the memory exists for me now. I packed my leather planner, soon to overflow with meetings, interviews, endless interviews. I collected the envelope of payment from the mailbox at the end of the driveway, closed the front door one final time, and went off to claim my palimpsest career.

I do not drown. I come alive on the side of a large rock, coughing up water that burns on its way back out and over my lips, holding hands with other rock dwellers, all of us flat on our backs and strapped in place under a large net.

"She's awake!" my rock neighbor says.

"What's happening?" I ask, my throat raw. "What's happening?"

"Don't strain your voice, dear."

"Who are you? Where am I?"

"You're on our rock, sweetie. You've been enlisted as a human barnacle by the Wildlife Preservation Initiative. Remember?"

My rock neighbor is an older woman with shells cluttering her hair. She notices me noticing her shells.

"I'm Barnacle Betty, but you can call me Joan. I'm trying to build a convincing crust."

Her shells extend through her braids, down her arms, and over her sandy, pruney hands, one of which encloses my palm in a delicate, crumbling carapace.

"We're filling in for a species on the brink of extinction!" says the man next to Barnacle Betty, or rather, Joan. "Coastal degradation," he adds.

"Oh?" I say, polite as ever, regaining a sense of geography, reality. A school of fish swims through my legs, tickling my ankles.

"I signed up on account of the rumors about barnacle dicks," he says.

"That's his way of saying he wants you to ask him about barnacle dicks," Joan, or Barnacle Betty, says, a wave splashing over her head.

"ok," I say, and I look at the man expectantly. "Tell me more."

The rock produces dozens of groans and sighs and not-agains. I tilt my head back and see human barnacles stretching out in the distance on our rock, which spans at least a hundred yards.

"Barnacles have the largest dicks in the animal kingdom. In relation to their size, I mean."

"It's good to keep your aspirations lofty," Joan says.

"Laugh all you want. I'm an ecological savior. The name's Harold, by the way." He turns to me. "But you can call me Barnacle Toby."

Joan squeezes my hand, and I look under her seaweed wreath and into her eyes.

"I signed up because barnacles don't have hearts," she whispers. "Mine beats fewer beats every day."

Small waves beat against my thighs. The sun beats down hard, and I hear seagulls in the distance. Beats marking out music. Music and voices and sunscreen. We're not far from shore.

"The thing is," I explain, for anyone listening, "you signed up for this job, but I did not. At least, I don't think I did. I don't remember."

"What?" says Joan. "Of course you did! We were expecting the new arrival yesterday, and there you were, pretty as a picture, floating toward our rock."

"I walked the plank of a pirate ship. Your misunderstanding saved my life."

Joan smiles but seems concerned. We hold our breath for a wave.

"If you're not supposed to be here," she asks, "then who is?"

I imagine a would-be human barnacle sinking to the bottom of the sea for want of a rock. Joan and Barnacle Toby must imagine something similar, because they grow as silent as their chosen species.

"I need to speak to my agency," I say, but my voice trails off at the end. There's not much hope for a phone.

"Well," Barnacle Toby says, "you'll get paid just like the rest of us. No different than filling in and growing roots at a desk, really. Might as well stick around."

I haven't known many human barnacles in my life. I haven't known many people who stick around. The thing I admire about the arthropods is the way they live in small, crispy houses and cement their houses to sturdy spots for good. When and if they break away, the foundation of the house stays put, so strong is their natural adhesive.

"One day I'll be promoted," says Joan. "I'll be the barnacle that rides the back of a whale. A special kind of breed."

In the distance we see other rocks, other people filling in for other species. Barnacle Toby points out the mussels, the clams, the whelks, a woman struggling, desperate to shrink into a shell. And farther in the distance still, halfway around the world, the reef that stopped living long ago, now renewed with life, a species replaced, then another, another. People earning a living perched on the dead coral, adapting and developing new, aquatic characteristics. One man claims his hand has sprouted a hard, pink skeleton, or so I'm told. A temporary evolution.

"It's the least we can do," says Barnacle Toby, who in his former life was known as Harold. The new name uses his new species as a title, as if to speak his new identity into existence, and I wonder, if he had been called Human Harold, if we were all addressed as Human first, would it somehow enforce our humanity? And when we're gone, will there be anyone left to fill in?

"Nice necklace," Joan says, and I realize I've completely forgotten my possessions. But there they are, taped to my chest. My eye patch still covers my eye, adjusting my vision for every change in light.

Low tide, and the water leaves us for a moment. So this is it, I think. This is where I stay, facing south until the end of time. How long is the lifespan of a barnacle? I ask, but I forget to ask out loud. I'm already turning silent and still, the species rising within me, the tide rising once more. Perhaps my tongue has already stuck to the sides of my mouth, hardening into a single layer of flesh, urging my body into the creature I'm meant to be.

Evening falls on a sleeping layer of human barnacles, and I hear a splash near our rock. Another splash, and a sigh of relief.

"There you are," says the man who, in another life, I knew as a parrot. "I've been looking for you."

He cuts me free and, kicking under the cover of night, gently swims us ashore.

We wash up on a beach, and the man with the long hair says, "This is where I'm from. I've brought you here to start your next placement."

He lets me cough up brine and dump plankton from my stolen boots. He untangles algae from my necklace.

"My necklace," I gasp, and I check that the Chairman remains intact.

He escorts me to a phone so I can confirm my new assignment with Farren. We trudge past abandoned anchors in the harbor and I think, This isn't a place that books round-trip tickets.

"Farren?" I say. "I've completed my assignment."

We stand at a pay phone on a deserted road. The man squeezes out his long hair onto the gravel until he stands in a small body of water.

"Oh, that's great to hear!" Farren says. The sound of her voice is such a relief, I nearly start to sob. "They were very pleased with you, missy," she says with a laugh.

"Thanks for the feedback, Farren. Really, thanks."

"Don't forget to update your resume."

"I won't," I say, wiping my eyes. "I'm a stickler."

"And your time sheets?"

"I'm a stickler for time sheets too."

"Yes, that's why you're in such high demand."

"I'm in high demand?" I ask, sniffling a little. *Something in my eye*, I mouth to the man with the long hair.

"Sure you are!"

"How nice," I say.

"That's right. It's nice to be wanted. It's nice to be needed. It's nice to punch a card with the world every morning, to let the world know you're still alive and punching and kicking. You're surely bound for the steadiness!"

"Farren, I hate to be a bother, but could you look into collecting payment for me from the Wildlife Preservation Initiative?"

"Of course, sugar. You bring the sugar. I'll handle the direct deposit. So enterprising, you."

"Also, how are you today?" I ask.

"How am I? I don't understand."

"What have you been up to?"

"Life. I've been up to life. It's none of your business," Farren says, her voice suddenly clipped. Then, "Oh, you know, non-disclosures is what I meant, and so forth."

"Of course," I say. "But what color are your nails today?"

"Blue," she says.

Blue.

"Aquamarine," she says.

"Oh, and Farren?"

"What is it, superstar?"

"It's just . . . I miss you," I say.

"What's that?"

"Nothing, nothing. Just thank you so much. Thank you so much. Thank you so, so much," I say. "So, so much."

"Just doing my job," she says. "You know that, right?"

"Right. Me too."

Farren instructs me on where to go next. The man with the long twisty hair, it turns out, is my new employer. He takes temporary jobs when work gets slow, which explains his gig as the parrot, Maurice.

"Times like these," he says.

I understand.

He has a few more quarters for me, so I call the boyfriends. Specifically, I call my culinary boyfriend.

"Food systems analyst," my culinary boyfriend says, correcting me.

"That's news to me," I say.

"I guess so. You've been gone!"

It turns out they're at my apartment again, the boyfriends, sitting around my old coffee table, a red oval slab with hairpin legs that I found on the side of the street and hauled upstairs all by myself.

"Really?" I ask. "What are you doing?"

They've started a book club. My culinary boyfriend brings the snacks. *Food systems analyst!* he yells in the background. The phone fills with clouds of laughter.

"Today," he says, "I made a duck liver hors d'oeuvre, a foamed grapefruit amuse-bouche, and a cheesy puff shareable plate."

When my culinary boyfriend used to cook for me, it was a shareable plate of takeout, and when I say plate, I really mean carton.

"Also," he says, "you got another letter about the stolen boots. Your former employer implores you to return her boots, promptly and without a struggle."

"Thanks for mentioning it," I say.

"She'll garnish your shoes for the rest of your life unless you return her boots in passable condition."

"Got it."

"She will break into your apartment while you are sleeping and take half of each pair of shoes under the glorious shroud of night, and when you wake up, you will have only single, solitary shoes to mark your singular, lonely life," he says. "I'm just quoting!"

My earnest boyfriend grabs the phone.

"I put all the spiders on the window ledge!" he says. "Even the tiny ones!"

"That's great, love."

"Book club is the best," he says, audibly beaming, without a hint of sarcasm. I think I hear him tumble forward into a pile of boyfriends, maybe on the couch, and they laugh and scream like fiends. Are they tickling one another?

My turn, I hear. No, mine, I hear. Give me the phone! Me next! Oh, you!

"We're reading a novel," says my favorite boyfriend, rising from the chaos, "about a group of friends just like ours. They have fights and disagreements, but they love each other until the end of time, which for all they know might be just around the corner. Some of the friends move away, but the people who move away are instantly forgotten. The story's lyrical and told in the style of a really great song, like that one we heard at that concert all those years ago. I won't spoil the ending. But everyone dies! You would love it. Maybe you'll read it, hon?"

I remember my favorite boyfriend snickering at my book clubs and knitting circles, and I wonder why his is any different. Why is yours different? I don't ask.

The food systems analyst says all of them will be friends for life, these boyfriends. I've built something lasting for them, something they can count on.

"You don't even know what you've given us," he says, his voice trembling. "You could not even possibly know."

Blood Work

The long-haired man is named Carl, and he's something of an entrepreneur. His small murder business sits in a tidy shack not far from the water. Convenient for dumping bodies.

"Location, location, location," he says.

"You sound like my real estate boyfriend!" I laugh.

Every morning I wash Carl's weapons, adhering to the cleaning manual he developed. I'm filling in for his buddy who's currently serving some time. Carl doesn't always pay in money, but he feeds me and gives me a place to sleep, a small cot next to his desk in the shack, where I hide my possessions under the mattress: my rubies, my eye patch, my brooch in the shape of a nautilus shell.

"I can offer you gobs of experience," he says.

"What about exposure?"

"I can offer you the opposite of that."

He promises me stock in his company. "When we go public, you'll be a very rich lady!"

Murder isn't a brand that usually goes public, I think, at least not by choice. But I don't dare turn up my nose at a share of his shares.

"You've got a knack," he says, making a sound like *knack* with a crack of his fingers. It warms my damn heart. Carl warms my heart in general. It feels grand to see him in his element.

"I'm sorry we weren't friendlier on the ship," I say.

"Nothing to be sorry for," he says, "is my motto." He hands me a beer on the roof of his shack, where we sit and smoke and watch the sun set over the sea.

I take initiative from the get-go and amortize the cost of Carl's assassination equipment.

"This one is cheaper," I say, shopping for spears. "Sharpener included, free with purchase!"

He's grateful when I help him approach his daily schedule with more efficiency, and sometimes he lets me assist in planning the logistics of the murders.

"If you take this street," I point out, "you'll shave six minutes off the getaway."

"Well, I never!"

"Just a slight detour. No more nick of time."

"I'll have a second to stop for a sandwich even," he says. "Thanks, kid."

He comes home holding an artisan panini, and I see the gratitude all over his face.

Carl schedules the kills for Tuesdays through Thursdays so he can take long weekends. He comes home on a Wednesday and I know where he's been: knocking off a gentleman in the center of the city.

"Gentle's debatable," he says. "Man: also debatable. More like a monster, really."

These are the only kinds of details he ever offers, the kind stripped from the innards of context I've already been given.

An elderly woman in a sixth-floor walk-up: as high and mighty as her apartment! A child on horseback: less kid and more cavalry!

He walks inside and first thing removes his shoes, pants, and shirt, and everything underneath, and balls up the clothing in a nylon bag he hangs on a hook near the door. He walks straight to the tub and runs the water until a stratus of steam seeps from the bathroom and into the living space. We don't discuss the murders, or, as Carl calls them, the business trips. While he enjoys his bath, I take the nylon bag and douse it in bleach. I wash the whites and colors in cold, crisp water. I take a dryer sheet and set it on my forehead like a veil, then lean forward and slip the sheet down my nose and into the machine with the fresh, clean clothes. If there's a stain I can't scrub, we snip the fabric in the trouble spot: a shirt with holes is better than a shirt with evidence. I prepare a bowl-sized cup of chamomile, and I set it on his desk with a plate of cookies near his journal, where he records the minutes and seconds from the end of every life he takes.

"Those moments are sacred," he says, toweling off his hair. "Don't think I don't know how to declare a time of death."

"I didn't think. I don't know."

"That's why I write it down, see," he says, jabbing the book with his finger. "It would be imprudent to forget. I'm trying to be better about keeping company records, kiddo."

"Can I help?"

"I'm sure you can. But it's my job, not yours. And anyway, plausible deniability."

We find a rhythm in this routine. Summer is the busy season, and Carl is all booked up. "Something about the heat," he says, "makes the blood boil." He comes home on a Tuesday, removes his shoes, pants, and shirt, balls them up in the nylon bag, and runs the water for his bath. I do the wash and fold the socks and prepare the chamomile and the cookies, and Carl stays up most of the night recording the intricacies of the murder of a young bank robber named Laurette, who kept receipts from every robbery like she was preparing to do her taxes. Instead of the taxes, she's the one who got done. Carl is writing when the sun is rising, and then it's coffee and a bagel and a schmear and off to prepare for the next day's slaughter.

I know about Laurette because Carl keeps his journal on his desk. While he's gone, what else can I do but take a peek? I peek on a regular basis. I know about a lot of people now, not just Laurette. Research, I tell myself. How can I be of assistance without a clear context for the work? How can I be of clear conscience without knowing what clouds the conscience to begin with?

Only once does Carl come home and break his habits. He walks into the shack with his shoes still laced, tracks blood and mud all over the floor. He slumps in a chair, still wearing his business garb. I'm not sure what to do, so I just listen as he explains the feeling of knife hitting bone, the sound of the crack of a neck, and how it reminds him of the sound of holiday crackers bursting at a fancy dinner table.

"Your table?" I ask.

"No," he says. "I'm not sure whose. I'm not sure where that memory's from. I'm not even sure it's mine."

"I understand," I say. I unbutton his shirt and help him out of his shoes, and I clean the shack until it shines.

On Sundays, I have free time to explore the place Carl calls home, and I find that I love it quite a bit. I love the weather and the people who sit near the dock. I love my job. Files and documents come and go by way of the shredder, but murder is a task that lasts. It's nice to have my head in something nearly steady. I'm not sure if the real steadiness will come, but a girl can dream.

I frequently stop at the cart that sells shaved ice drizzled with lemon and cherry, and I eat the ice with a wooden spoon, staining my tongue red and yellow, sitting on the boardwalk watching the sea, looking for human barnacles, starfish, jellyfish populating the shore. I like to find the shells with tiny holes punched at the tops, perfect for holding the length of a chain. I slip a glowing mother-of-pearl specimen on my necklace, to keep the Chairman company, and the name of the shell contains the names of two of my favorite people. My necklace feels like a little family, for want of a picture in a locket.

In the evening, Carl takes me to the carnival, where we ride the carousel at least ten times. Porcelain horses. More like cavalry, I think.

"Don't you feel dizzy?" he shouts.

"I feel excellent!"

We play the midway games, and he's proficient in the

challenge where you shoot a dart at a rising balloon.

"Gotcha," he says, and he gets it several times. Every now and then, someone stops and stares—not only to admire his marksmanship. They watch him with expressions I've never seen before, and I say, Carl, let's go, let's please go, let's leave now, let's please go now, before they have a chance to turn their expressions into something worse, to reach in their pockets, to pull back their coats, to slip a hand into a boot or reveal a holster strapped to a belt. These are, of course, I think, Carl's victims come to haunt him, come to claim revenge, left to pick up the pieces of his various business trips. Or maybe they aren't, or maybe they are, or maybe they just ate some bad funnel cake. I'll never know; I never do find out. Life is a stranger in a crowd whose intentions are unclear and, come to think of it, so is death.

Carl wins a cornucopia of stuffed animals for me, a litter of toxic-green inanimate bunnies. He carries my prizes so I can hold my drink and walk unencumbered, swinging my arms and spinning my skirt, and when I get tired, he carries me as well, sets me on the cot to sleep, lifts my legs under the covers. I wake up in what feels like a soft rabbit warren, surrounded by the plush, sweet gifts from the night before.

Other nights, my sleep isn't as sound, and the necklace takes hold. The Chairman and I travel the length of the shore and back again, my feet bloodied by sharp shells. We climb the lifeguard chair, the scaffolding under the boardwalk, the water tower, the carnival Ferris wheel. We talk about life, about business, about decisions related to both. Carl finds me climbing his shack in the hours before dawn, talking to myself, and I explain the effects of my necklace.

"Does he have good advice?" he asks, bandaging my feet.

"Good, but maybe misplaced?"

"I used to watch you talking to yourself on the pirate ship," Carl says, and I remember all the times I watched him from afar myself. I'm so glad we have something in common. I take the common ground and turn it into a site on which to plant the rest of our days. "Remember when we kept tabs on each other?" we'll say. "Remember when we took those tabs and settled them up?" I think of his socks, folding them in little packages. I think of how many times I've seen him walk naked from the door to the tub. I think of the elegant, sturdy block letters filling the pages of his journal. I could ask him to become one of my boyfriends, even though I haven't added a new boyfriend in ages, let alone a long-distance one. Then I think of my other boyfriends nestled at home, the distance something I hadn't considered before. These days, all my boyfriends are long-distance. But then again, so is the length of an arm stretched between two people watching each other from afar.

"Do you want to be one of my boyfriends?" I ask.

"That's not in my skill set, kid," Carl says, and he gives me a long, soft kiss good-night.

The full story of Laurette the bank robber is complicated indeed. Carl wrote ten pages in his murder journal about how he was and always will be filled with regret and sorrow for what happened, even though his motto is "Nothing to be sorry for," and how if he could take it back he would, because the girl who robbed the bank that day, the girl who stole the money at the hour Carl had set the murder on his schedule, she wasn't Laurette, she was a substitute bank robber with a penchant for bright face masks and bright gloves, and she wore a floral mask that complemented her blue eyes, and Carl knew right away when her eyes hung open after she had left her body that no, this wasn't Laurette at all, for in her file it clearly stated that Laurette had silver eyes, not blue, and he ripped off the mask and there, from her limp, slack face, he got the full proof he was dreading. He had gone and murdered the wrong person.

On the day in question, Laurette herself was home with the flu and a fever of 102 and a stack of magazines and reruns from her favorite television programs and a well-received documentary about the true lives of Bonnie and Clyde, which she'd been saving for a special occasion. She felt lucky to have coverage on her sick day, and that word, *coverage*, was a word she liked—the shirt that covered her shoulders, the blanket that covered her body, the sleep hat that covered her head, the roof that covered her hat, the sky that covered her roof, the universe that always covered her ass, so lucky was she. Lucky Laurette. Her fever was so high she started to hallucinate that the robbery hadn't gone as planned, that something was wrong at the bank, and that her younger sister, who had filled in for her that day, was standing before her near the couch, wearing her favorite floral mask, begging her to come and help.

"The heist is a bust," her younger sister said, or so Laurette thought.

"A bust is just a heist performed by your body," Laurette said, and when she heard her own voice out loud she knew she was delirious, and she fell asleep there on the couch with a magazine in her lap opened to an article about how no one really wears the correct bra size, not really, not ever.

Word reached Laurette late that night, the news on the television, someone tried to rob a bank, someone was dead, the robber was dead, body missing, and Carl stood outside her house watching her through the window, and she was at once bewildered and devastated. She started laughing hysterically, like a woman who stands under a piano falling from the sky, and the piano misses her by inches, and then the realization of a life spared fills her with maniacal giggles. Then she started crying, like a woman who realizes that even though the piano didn't fall on her head, it fell on someone else's head instead, and not just any someone, but her younger sister, a brilliant bank robber in her own right with so much potential, so much potential, potential like a piano prodigy, and she suddenly hated the word *potential*, because it's either wasted or lived up to and guess who was no longer up to living in this particular scenario.

The universe had covered Laurette's ass yet again. The universe! The universe doesn't subtract, it just replaces. Matter isn't created or destroyed, it's just replaced, it just changes, it's just misplaced. And if nothing is ever really lost, how can we ever mourn? That's what Laurette wanted to know. Laurette laughed and cried and laughed and cried and thought about that word, *coverage*, and how it reminded her of the word *shroud*, and how it also described the *grief* that now covered her entire life, and she turned off the television and went to open the window for some fresh air, and there was Carl, standing in the twilight, watching her. A lesser woman might have screamed, but Laurette hadn't been startled in upward of twenty years, and all she said was, "Why not join me inside?" For she knew he was certainly death, come at last to collect.

This part Carl wrote about in great detail. He wrote about taking Laurette's temperature with a thermometer, now one hundred flat, as though the experience of loss had broken her fever. By some miracle, she was letting him care for her. He made her a cold compress for her head and put ice packs around her body on the couch, put some soup on the stove, warmed the broth so it was just barely hot, and spooned it through Laurette's dry lips, and pulled the blanket to her chin, and sat down next to her. Laurette was small, and they could fit on the tiny couch together without even touching,

Laurette lying down, legs stretched out all the way.

"Are you here to kill me with poisoned soup?" Laurette asked, and Carl explained that no, he couldn't take two lives in one night, it was bad for his constitution, and bad for the world, and since he'd disposed of her sister's body, for all anyone knew, it was Laurette who was killed that night and not her sister, and no one ever had to know about this discrepancy, especially not the people who had hired Carl to kill Laurette, and Laurette could go on robbing banks and no one would ever on their lives suspect a lady, this lady, she who according to the facts was already deader than dead.

Laurette stayed silent for a bit. Then, "Who hired you to kill me?"

Carl wasn't supposed to reveal information like this, especially not to the people meant to be murdered, but he was in a revelatory mood, and he considered all those movies where the villain tells the captive the entire evil plan before executing said evil plan, and so maybe there was a tradition, a precedent that allowed for such bravado, and of course in this scenario they were both villains, a fact Carl and Laurette had each come to terms with in their own way, in their own time, long, long ago.

"The banks hired me," Carl says.

"But the banks hired me to rob the other banks!" Laurette said. "And then the other banks hired me to rob the robbing banks in retaliation!"

"Maybe the banks are all the same bank? Just one big bank," Carl hypothesized, and Laurette let this idea sink in for a minute: Maybe the banks are all the same bank. Maybe the people are all the same people. Maybe I'm my sister and my sister is me, and in this way, living is also a state of mourning. She noticed she was feeling a little better, sweat shining on her forehead. She helped herself to a sip of soup, and then she remembered her sister again, and a different fever set in. She remembered when they were little girls playing cops and robbers, and no one wanted to play the cop, so they asked an actual officer of the law to join them in their game, both for the sake of verisimilitude and necessity, and he played at being himself, and he trained them real good in justice and law enforcement and how to do the opposite, and he contributed to their future in ways he probably hadn't expected. They all learned a lot that summer.

And then Carl made more soup. And then he and Laurette watched the Bonnie and Clyde documentary. And then they talked shop, their chosen professions, their jobs, no, their careers, for they found solace in this necessary work, and how when every other door had closed to them, these doors had opened, and beggars can't be choosers, and isn't that just the way you find your purpose sometimes, by looking into the last available option and meeting your sorry self, standing there at the end of the line?

"Can you take me to her body?" Laurette asked.

"Sort of," Carl said, and he wrapped her in a quilt and led her through the city and past the harbor and down to the public beach, where the waves slipped forward and back and over the sand. I was waiting nearby in the murder shack, preparing cookies and chamomile, not knowing Carl stood just outside the door with the woman he was meant to kill.

"Your sister's out there with the rest of the bodies," said Carl, waving his hand toward the ocean.

Laurette stood by the grave and wept for her sister, for the other people Carl had murdered, for the people murdered by people other than Carl, for the people who murdered each other, bang, bang, for the people lost at sea, for the people on planes who crashed from the sky and into the water, for the people who were supposed to be on those planes but who changed their tickets and were spared, only to end up on different planes, still crashing into the water, crashing into icebergs, crashing into the people who stayed home from work and weren't crashed into by planes, but who then tied bricks to their ankles and threw themselves to the bottom of the sea and crashed into other people crashing to their deaths, for the exploding cruises and the wayward sailors lured by sirens, for the people who lived in places where once upon a time there used to be cities but now the cities were completely underwater, and then an image came into her mind of the bodies drifting in the ocean like so much debris, detritus, the dead, the flotsam and jetsam floating together like magnets, like a giant buoy of bodies, like a bridge, irresistible, like the original land bridge that led Earth's ancestors across the ocean, like a new kind of land that washes together into a new kind of continent, forming new kinds of mountains and new kinds of fields and a geography the likes of which we've never seen, a desert that looks like a torso and a forest of trees that look like heads of hair, and the bodies unite to form a rare kind of matter with enough continental drift, with enough momentum, with enough coverage to cover the entire world, replace it clean and fresh and new, and so in this way, Laurette thought, maybe we can finally start over.

Carl eventually asks me to join him on a kill. I'm sitting on my cot and he's sitting at his desk. I've felt this moment coming for a while now. Initially I thought it was romance, but we had our long, soft kiss, and I put that memory in the bottom of my purse for a rainy day, and that romance between us turned into something else. What I'm experiencing here isn't hearts and roses, but the romance in the promise of a shared skill. Carl has taken to instructing me on the grip one grabs around a knife, the way to lift a sledgehammer from the knees and not the shoulders, the respectable application of poison. One doesn't want to be gauche when administering poison, Carl says. Don't overdo it. It needs to look pleasant, accidental.

And now, he says, I'm ready.

"Are you sure about this, Carl?"

"I know you'll be aces!" he says, slapping my leg. "The perfect sidekick. Just picture it!"

"I need to think," I say. I think about whether or not I can do this with my bare hands, then return home and touch my bare hand against my favorite boyfriend's cheek, put my bare hand in my pocket, use my fingers to flip through every memory I have, changing the memories with each murderous swipe.

"Usually," he says, "I wear gloves."

Does that change anything? Maybe it does. Planning a killing is one thing, but the execution is a different story.

"It's not like you don't have any experience," Carl says. "Give yourself some credit, golly. After all, you decapitated the imposter Pearl on the pirate ship. All by yourself, no less! I won't soon forget that legendary kill. No one will."

"Very true," I say, and I'm disturbed by his crystalline memory. Has he recorded my legendary kill in his book of kills? I feel dread rising in my throat. I remember hoisting the alleged Pearl over the side of the ship and slipping a life preserver around her waist.

I try to find comfort with lying every day, practicing mostly on myself.

"Was that your first?" he asks, and the question takes me by surprise.

"Yes, of course it was."

"I never presume to know," Carl says, and he leaves me to consider his offer.

I've been reading up on Carl's murders, and frankly, I don't know if I have what it takes. It takes a lot for me to admit my hesitation, and I don't take it lightly that I might not be cut out for certain kinds of work. This is a hard truth for a temp to face: I just might not be cut out for the life that comes with killing.

In Carl's murder journal, there are specific descriptions of the deaths, diagrams, details. Blunt instruments and burst eardrums, knives stuck through eyes and out the backs of heads.

Sometimes a woman will request the prospectus for a murder and make suggestions to Carl based on what she knows will cause the victim additional pain. Torture isn't a thing I'd considered. Sometimes a man will request the prospectus for a murder and make suggestions to Carl based on what he knows will cause the least pain possible. Sometimes the murders are merciful and sometimes they're not. Sometimes a man will add a detail that doesn't become pertinent until the end of the crime, like when Carl is instructed to reveal a daffodil right before he stabs the exposed gut, and the daffodil is a mystery to Carl, but a look of recognition washes over the victim's face at an appropriate interval, timed to coincide with death.

I sit on the boardwalk spooning my shaved ice, weighing the pros and cons. I used to stay up late making pro/con lists with my insurance salesman boyfriend, who practiced risk management on the side, balancing and testing every important decision. With hardly any prompting, the lists quickly devolved into nasty bits of literature about the other boyfriends—which one snores too much, which one drinks too much, which one might be the kind of boyfriend who someday marries me, which one might be the kind of boyfriend who someday hits me, which one might be the kind of boyfriend who someday gets eaten by his cats, which one has the biggest apartment, which one has the biggest hole in his heart. We would fall asleep on a pile of papers and I would wake up with a headache and a stomachache and a bitch hangover, which is the kind of hangover you get in the morning after spending the whole night talking shit, saying crap, acting like a huge and massive jerk, allowing all the horrible things in your head to somehow make their slimy way out of your mouth.

Today, my pro/con list is a short one. Under the pro column: learn the new skill of murdering. Under the con column: whoops, now you've murdered. And I haven't really described Carl's full murder journal, the extent of it, the volumes, the pages and pages of imagery written with bright, inky pens, and most of all, the pages at the center of the book with nothing on them at all; actually I cannot say what was and wasn't written there because those pages have been ripped out. All that remains: a frayed, jagged seam peppered with torn paper dust. I scour the shack for the missing pages, and every time, I come up short, convinced they have long ago been turned to ocean pulp.

Carl says I won't have to do any of the dirty deeds at first. I can just do the administrative duties. Watching the door. Holding the bag of weapons, at first. Looking malicious, at first, then later, Carl says, eventually, demonstrating true internal malice. Carl wants my answer by the end of the week.

When Carl goes to eat an artisan panini with Laurette, I grab his journal and make haste toward the prison. I walk past the harbor and along the public beach, turning into the center of the city, walking through the city until the city fades into a copse of trees, a forest, and I haven't visited the forest before, not yet. I cross a stream and pass through a clearing, through several gates of wood and wire, through a metal detector and an intrigue detector and a sorrow detector and a new kind of detector that detects schemes, patent pending, and I sign the book with a fake name, and I say I've come to visit Carl's buddy, who is serving some serious time.

"I've come to visit Carl's buddy, who is serving some serious time."

I want to ask Carl's buddy about the missing pages.

"What can you tell me about this?" I ask him, and I open Carl's book.

"Carl won't like it," he says, "you looking at his book."

"Tough."

"Tough is right. Tough like me. I looked at his book too."

For the first time I smile, and he smiles, then a guard comes over to our table.

"We don't encourage that," he says, and we put our smiles away, and the guard goes away too. I put a pack of cigarettes on the table for Carl's buddy, to sweeten the deal.

"Those were the pages about me," Carl's buddy says, taking the cigarettes, and he strokes his beard with his thumb. "He destroyed the evidence. Shortened my sentence by ten years."

"I see."

"Protecting me forever, as best he can. That's Carl."

"All right."

"So now you know what I know. We both know the same knowledge. You know?"

I do know.

I leave Carl's buddy and wish him luck and hold my breath through the scheme detector, patent pending, the sorrow detector, the intrigue detector, and the metal detector and walk through several gates, through a clearing, and over a stream, through the forest I've now visited, back into the center of the city, past the harbor, and along the public beach, walking straight into Carl and Laurette on their way back to the shack, finishing their artisan paninis.

"OK, Carl," I say. "I'll do it."

"OK," says Carl, and he nods to Laurette, and Laurette nods back, and we're all standing there nodding in a small cluster of yes.

And so I agree to the murder less for murder's sake and more out of respect for Carl's loyalty, for his sturdy nature, in honor of his friendship with his buddy who is serving some time, because let's face it, that kind of friendship is worth killing for, worth serving time for, to say the least.

"OK," I say. "I'll do it. Who do I have to kill?"

And Carl says, "First, we train."

"And does she work with us now?" I ask, pointing at Laurette, the politest point I can muster. "Like, permanently?"

"Maybe," says Carl. "Is that OK?"

"Not for me to say, but probably it is. Sure, why not!"

Laurette gives me a sweet look from the other side of the shack, where she's making Carl's bed differently than the way I make it, with hospital corners and tight folds. What she doesn't know is that Carl likes to let one foot hang off the edge of the bed, untucked. Those sheets will be a mess by morning.

What Carl means when he says "First, we train" is that I'm going to shadow him for a time. I'm going to stand behind him and copy his motions, his emotions, his expressions. I'll be as silent as a shadow, dressed all in black, and Laurette lets me borrow a turtleneck and trousers to wear with my stolen boots.

"Looking good," she says, and I believe her.

I shadow Carl when he buys his artisan panini, taking shadow money from my shadow pocket, placing the payment on a shadow counter that sits just beyond the real counter. Afterward, sitting on a shadow bench behind Carl's bench and spreading my legs, spreading my shadow panini with a packet of shadow mayo and not even using a shadow knife, I shadow eat my shadow panini, but it tastes more like a plain old sandwich, full of shadows such as it is. Carl opens his mouth really wide, so I open my mouth really wide. He takes a big bite, so I take a big shadow bite. And were the bite not a shadow, it would be the kind of bite to make my mother say, "Small bites, or else you'll choke." Then Carl pulls a piece of lettuce off his lip, and you can call my shadows anything you want, but they certainly aren't messy shadows, so I skip the lettuce part.

We walk home under the setting sun, and Carl's actual shadow stretches long and thin and falls over my shadow face.

This goes on for some time. I sleep every night in a sleep shadow of Carl's sleep, which is just fine, because Laurette has claimed my cot for a while. My dreams shadow his dreams. I'm locked into the shadow life I'm leading. Sure enough, as predicted, Carl's foot pokes out from his sealed-up sheets, and I poke my foot out from beneath my shadow sheet, lying on the floor next to Carl.

One morning, he is standing over me as I'm just starting to wake. "Stage two," he says. "Now you'll be my mirror."

It's a more personal exercise, and there's nothing more

personal than doing my job. Eye contact and staying close together. We work around the shack, timing our movements, learning to move the same way. I wash my hair in the shower watching Carl wash his hair in the shower. He washes everything else watching me wash everything else, and we have different kinds of everything else, but otherwise, the mirror is perfect. Sometimes we touch bellies or elbows, the way you touch a mirror and are suddenly touching yourself, and I feel a shock go through my whole body, and I remember that soft, long kiss and feel pulled into a current, and one night Carl kisses his mirror, and his mirror kisses back while Laurette sleeps on my cot nearby, and the whole room vibrates like a reflection on a piece of billowing plastic.

"Hi," he says, and so do I.

This goes on for some time. I'm happy and bursting, and I have an excuse to look at Carl twenty-four hours a day, if I can stay awake that long, and Laurette just stands off to the side making us lasagna for the company we keep in our own little mirror world. We start to speak in unison, with varied success. I can't seem to keep my sentences in sync. Carl is understanding. "Let's switch to weapons," he says, and we swipe swords at the wall, spill poison in even pours, fastidious with the cleaning of our hands and scrubbing of other exposed surfaces.

Then it changes. I wake in Carl's bed and Carl is gone. He comes back later that day, hardly says a word to me.

"Carl?" I say, and Carl says nothing. I think I hear him give a short, clipped laugh, like a scoff, like a burp with resentment around the edges, but I can't be sure.

He goes for a walk with Laurette, and I pace the shack like a person gone mad. Maybe he knows I went to visit his buddy who's serving some serious time. Maybe he knows I read his journal. Maybe these things are unforgivable.

They come home late and I'm waiting by the door. "Carl? Laurette? Carl? Laurette?"

"Stage three, sweetheart," Laurette says, stroking my cheek. "We've found you someone to kill."

The person to be killed is tied up neatly in a vault at a bank where Laurette is still on good terms with the bank manager. That is where Carl and Laurette went on their walk, to tie up the victim and lock the victim inside the safe. He or she is waiting there for me to do what I said I would do, to perform my job, and that is the plan.

"Can I have more details?" I ask.

"No," says Carl, who hasn't looked me in the eye since we were mirrors. "Not this time."

We walk to the bank single file, and Laurette gives me the bag of weapons to carry. She slips Carl's murder journal in the bag, so he can record my efforts concurrent with the execution.

"It's like a trial run, sweetheart," Laurette says, "except it's not a run, it's a kill. And it's not a trial, it's a life."

My face goes dark.

"No pressure!" she says.

We walk past the harbor and the public beach and into the center of the city. We're fully exposed, yet no one really sees us. It's amazing. I feel slick and invisible. The sky's bright with stars, with flashing blue lights from planes, bleeping blue across the sky like Farren's aquamarine nails. Then through the doors of the bank, which Laurette can open without even breaking a sweat. Then through the metal detector, turned off, the scheme detector, patent pending, disconnected from the wall outlet. Through the empty bank lobby and back to the vault, to the safe, to the lock Laurette cracks as easily as knuckles.

And there, tied to a chair, surrounded by stacks of gold doubloons, I see the alleged Pearl. The Pearl I supposedly, allegedly, already killed.

"I thought you could finish what you started," says Carl, his voice as cold as the sea.

"But what?" I ask. "How?"

"Guess who also likes artisan paninis?" Carl says, pointing at this sweet prisoner Pearl. "Guess who I saw yesterday, when I went to get an extra panini, just for you?" he asks, pointing at Pearl once again, Pearl, who is always a prisoner.

"Guess whose body is still attached to her head?" Carl asks.

My face feels like it's on fire, and I don't know what to do with my hands. I don't know what to do at all. I don't know where to look. I look to Laurette for comfort, but her face is turned away, covered in a floral mask.

"I can't believe I thought we were the same," Carl says, cornering me. "I can't believe I heard something in you that echoed something in me."

For the first time in a long time, I notice the sheer breadth of his body, the sheer weight and height of him.

"And the worst part," he says, "is that you didn't do your job."

He puts a knife in my hand and a knife to my back, then pushes me toward a horrified Pearl, her mouth taped shut, her eyes apologizing and begging with every blink.

"I can't," I say, my whole body shaking. "I can't."

I can't, I say once more, but I don't say it out loud. The words stop somewhere inside me.

"I know," Carl says, his voice suddenly tender, and he leans forward and slits Pearl's throat.

I cover my eyes.

Allegedly, that's what happened.

That's what the court transcripts will say happened.

What I can tell you is that Carl didn't cut Pearl's throat. It was Laurette.

It was Laurette who slit Pearl's throat with one quick slice, who grabbed my arm and pushed me to the other side of the safe door and locked Carl and the dying Pearl inside, with his weapons, with his journal, slipped safely into his bag by Laurette, his journal detailing every single murder, every single last one.

The safe, like a snack pantry, like a catacomb, like a tomb, clutched and sealed.

"I'm sorry," said Laurette, turning the lock.

"But why?" asked Carl, banging on the door.

Laurette's eyes filled up behind her mask. "I miss my sister!" she shouted.

And the gears clicked closed with a thud.

And we're standing on a hill stacked with betrayals, and the betrayals are stacked so high they topple and spill over, and

I can hear Carl banging a distant bang until it's just a far-off tremble in my eardrum.

The next thing I know, Laurette makes a call.

The next thing I know, I'm standing on the street. Sirens in the distance.

The next thing I know, I'm receiving a hug. I'm hearing the word *run*. Run like it's your job.

The next thing I know, Laurette is gone, and police cars are pulling around the block.

The next thing I know, I'm sitting in the murder shack. My things are in a bag, my eye patch, my rubies, my brooch in the shape of a nautilus shell, the same shape found in the spiral of a hurricane.

The next thing I know, I know I just watched someone die, and that someone was a person named Pearl, and so a little piece of my friend Pearl has died too.

The next thing I know, I don't know a single thing, not anymore.

I walk down a deserted road, wide awake. I find a pay phone and I make a call.

"Well, superstar," Farren says, "you've really done it this time."

"I hate disappointing you, Farren," I say. "I hate disappointing you the most."

"It's just, you were doing so great. Such a shame! Explain it to me one more time?"

"Carl's in jail."

"Right! Right. And you left your position without being discharged?"

"That's right."

"As in, no one discharged you?"

"That's right."

"So, here's the thing: I *am* disappointed. Really disappointed."

"Can you please give me a new placement?"

"I can't give you anything!" Farren laughs, then sighs. "Honey," and I can hear her nails tapping at her desk, the phone cord twisting around her index finger, "I shouldn't have even taken this call." The last part is whispered and low. I hope maybe the softness in her voice is a window to my future, a decibel I can climb through and use to make things right.

"How can I fix this?" I ask. "I can fix this!"

"This botched assignment truly botches things up. You feel me?"

"I feel you."

"Oh, I don't think you do."

"Just tell me what to do and I'll do it, Farren. I'll do anything. You know me, I'm a stickler."

"Then stick yourself back in time and make this disaster not happen. You've surely derailed yourself on the road to the steadiness."

"I have?"

"Girl, please. Abandoning a placement? Criminal activity without the prescribed levels of discretion? I don't know, maybe fifteen demerits? Maybe more?"

"Oh no. No, no, no."

"Now look, don't cry, don't cry, please," Farren says. "You know the procedure for fugitive temps. Right, honey?"

"I do."

"Good. Consult your leather planner and follow the rules. I've got to be going." Farren covers the phone and shouts to someone in the distance, "Pizza sounds perfect!"

"Wait. Wait just a minute," I say.

"I'm afraid I can't talk to you due to this truly botched assignment! We can't put the agency in danger, you know?"

"I know."

"It's of the utmost importance that I protect the agency, understand?"

"I understand."

"So don't call me anytime soon. Don't send me any time

cards, don't send me any birthday cards. Just go away. Go away. Go away. OK now?"

Farren covers the phone again and shouts, "Always pepperoni, obviously!"

And whispers to me, "I'll try to be in touch."

That decibel, and my hope returns. "How will you find me?" I ask in the same whisper.

"How does anyone find anyone in this infinite world?" she responds. And then, "Fine, so just do half with veggies!"

Before hanging up, there's a short pause, a fissure. It could be nothing, but I choose to hear it as hesitation. I fill it with the rest of Farren's day: Her pizza, her veggies, her meat, her sustenance, her nails buried in cheese and flaked in flour. Her colleagues laughing and kidding around. Huddling, as they say. "Let's have a morning huddle," they say, and they gather with arms wrapped around shoulders and hoist Farren in the air in her ergonomic chair. She crosses her legs. "You guys!" she says. "Here's a raise!" they say. "Get it? Because we're raising you in the air?" "I get it!" says Farren.

The office expands to the size of my desperation, and Farren is instantly a speck in an open-plan universe. And the universe populates itself with Farren's hopes, her dreams, her aspirations. Where does she go at five o'clock? She goes wherever she goddamn wants! The subway platform stretches before her like a runway and carries her to her door, her home, her apartment filled with children, no, with cats, no, with drawers and drawers and drawers of nail polish. Organized by color, just the way she saw it in a magazine. I can picture it. She sits at her self-care station near a window with billowing curtains, and she lights a candle, fir tree scented, smooths a dollop of moisturizer into her palms, paints each nail with a bottom layer of lacquer to protect her cuticle, then a thin coat of granite-colored polish, then a second coat, and then a third layer on her thumbs, achieving a presentable thumbs-up for her positive work in the world. Then a top coat to seal everything in place, and her hands stretched before her like a magician, palms down, rotating her wrists to chase the breeze of the oscillating fan. There's a certain power in this voluntary immobility, Farren thinks, smiling. I don't have to move if I don't want to! My hands are as soft as my sheets! I take care of myself, she thinks. She turns her hands over and over, bends her paws, practices the calisthenics required for the distribution of gainful employment. She collects dexterity like a precious alloy. She enchants the room to give her everything she has ever wanted, and the room delivers her favorite television program, fetches her a drink. And then the journal bookmarked with an inky purple pen, where Farren writes the story of her life, not wondering whether her life is a story at all, just taking it for granted as a plot that makes sense. "Today I woke up," she writes, and she proceeds with the clarity of an honest-to-god real person whose days unfold according to logic and precision. "I am a real person!" she writes, and so it must be true. "Today I abandoned a friend," she doesn't write, not remembering our call, just marking it as one of many disappointments, a series of disappointments, ill-advised investments of Farren's confidence and time. A folder of women with my shortcomings, my experiences, my failures. "Today I ate pizza," Farren writes, "and I felt satisfied."

When her nails are tough and dry, she sits on the floor in sweatpants, assesses her life choices, enumerates her achievements, flirts with a pile of resumes, finds someone to replace me.

I wish I had a criminal boyfriend to call, but I do not. I settle on a bench pushed up against the pay phone. I settle on my pacifist boyfriend, with whom I've never had a quarrel. He answers his phone and sounds out of breath but happy.

"Oh my gosh," he says. "Speak of the devil!"

"I'm the devil now?"

"Don't get confrontational, babe. It's just a turn of phrase!"

"OK then." You can turn a phrase only so many times before it turns into something else.

"Guess what?" he says. "You'll never guess. Never, never, never. Oh boy."

"What is it? Are you all right?" I can't take another shock to my heart, my head, to anything, really.

"I'm fine! Everyone's fine."

"Everyone?"

"That's right. We're all here at the Hangout for a very special occasion."

"What's the Hangout?" I ask, but I already know.

"Oh, we started calling your apartment the Hangout. We were tired of saying 'your apartment.' It gave us zero ownership over this place, which we treat so very, very nicely. So we turned the phrase around, and now we call it the Hangout!

Which has a pleasant ring to it! And also it describes what we do here! Which is mostly hanging out. But sometimes one of us will buy a new plant for a corner, or paint an accent wall, or hang some erotic photography, or put a broken coffee table on the sidewalk with a sign that says FREE, or replace that broken mug that says Favorite Mug, or break another mug for good measure so there are always an even number of mugs, or move the television to a different corner, or roll up a rug that doesn't really match, or catch a mouse under the rug, or keep the mouse as a pet, or hang a life coaching poster above the couch, or move the couch into the kitchen, or send our magazine subscriptions to this address, or send our groceries to this address, or have a stoop sale at this address, or throw away any objects that aren't currently in use at this address."

"The objects aren't currently in use," I say, "because their owner is *away.*"

I remember my pacifist boyfriend tidying my apartment in the past. I showed him how I liked the pillows on the couch to look, because I'm not particular about many things, but I'm particular about pillows.

"Show me!" he said, all tactical consensus.

I showed him how I liked the two small yellow pillows to rest on a diagonal against the large, soft, feathery pillow, buttons facing out. I centered them against the tufted cushion and draped a crocheted throw across the back of the sofa. When my pacifist boyfriend tried to replicate this staging, he invariably lined the pillows up like soldiers, which I found ironic for a pacifist. There they stood, straight against the tufted cushion, single file, tags popping from their corners like little white flags. And though his forgery in no way resembled my preferred pillow arrangement, the distance between our interpretations somehow made my chest swell, for his effort, for the aching separation between his intended outcome and the actual result, fueled only by the goodness in his heart.

"Also," he says, "we got a lizard!"

I can feel the pacifism retreating over some distant hill behind my eyes. "You had some news," I remind him. "Exciting news."

"Right! Right! Well . . ."

In the background I hear noisemakers, singing, clapping.

He says, "We turned your closet into an office!"

My handy boyfriend grabs the phone. "As a way of saying thanks!" he says, his voice a trill of muscular assembly.

"We stayed up all night working!" my caffeinated boyfriend chirps.

"Now you have a desk where you can leave your mug forever," my tallest guy says. "Although not the mug that says Favorite Mug. No one knows where that mug went. Don't ask about that mug."

I hear their arms around each other, their cheeks pressed to cheeks, phone sandwiched in the middle. I hear their pride, and something else too. I wonder who will use the desk while I'm away, or if the use of the desk even matters. Will the pet lizard lounge across the desk during my sabbatical from home? No, it's not the desk at all, it's the project that counts. I hear the inside jokes from their night of renovation, and I don't understand a single one. This is like a surprise party where they forget to invite the surprised party. They reminisce about shopping for donuts, picking out streamers. The piñata, the balloons. The party expands and replaces the person.

"Does the office have your blessing?" asks my favorite boyfriend.

"Of course it does. How nice. How actually very, very nice. I'm speechless. You guys."

"Now you have a chair and a lamp and a stack of papers!" says my favorite boyfriend. "Now you have a place to keep pens!"

My closet stretches back an extra square foot into the wall, a hidden crevice, a false exit. If you look deep enough inside a person, you'll see a surplus square foot, an elbowed bracket that extends past the boundaries of the body, and this is where you find the soul. My soul, now full of office supplies.

"What else?" I ask my favorite boyfriend.

"Just yesterday," he says, "your former employer came back and stole some of your shoes, because she insists you're still wearing her boots. She is convinced that her boots are on your ungrateful feet, your horrible deceitful indelicate feet. Just quoting. She started to cry, so we offered her a cup of tea from your Favorite Mug. We offered her an ottoman, and she kicked her moccasins off and stretched her toes against the fabric. She touched every book on your shelf. She told us some great stories about the new girl who organizes her shoes, a young intern with laudable personal hygiene. She complimented your tea selection. She smashed your Favorite Mug against the floor. She was very not OK. We let her steal a handful of your clogs. It totally made more room for your office!"

"What else?"

"We threw away our old fuzzy sweaters. They don't fit. We hate them. Now we wear denim jackets. We threw away an old bag stuffed with other bags, with little plastic bags balled inside the medium-sized paper bags. We threw away a skirt with a slit that ripped all the way to the top. We threw away a box in the back of your closet that was filled with nothing but human dust."

I throw the phone against its cradle and throw my hands in the air. I throw myself into a jog that lasts for days. I throw one leg in front of the other and throw my arms back and forth. I throw away the idea of sleep, but the necklace burns around my neck, and the Chairman throws himself into running beside me. We throw ourselves across the public beach, into the center of the city, through the forest, over the stream, and up to a discreet-looking building, no bells or whistles, no chimes or awnings, no signs or signals or warm welcomes. I climb the stairs and enter the agency for fugitive temps.

The First Temporary was assigned to complete a variety of projects.

"Burn this bush," one god said, and so she did.

"Now put the bush back the way it was," another god said, and so she learned the drudgery of tasks done and undone, the brutal makings and unmakings of the earth.

"Create an animal so rare it barely exists," the gods said. The First Temp cobbled together something extraordinary, irreplaceable.

"Someone," she corrected them.

"Now watch it go extinct," they said, and so she held its wing and watched it glimmer, fade, disappear.

Memory Work

When I was very young, I performed chores instead of jobs. I mopped the square footage and dusted the ledges but not in that order. Mind you, I was not so young as to let muck fall free and stick to soapy floors. I put away my toys and put away my dolls, and took them out and put them back again. The taking out and the putting away. I learned to cook brisket with sauce, and I learned to eat it. My mother held my hand and helped me slice the meat against the grain. "Small bites, or else you'll choke," she said.

The apartment smelled like a holiday. I cleared the dishes for my mother and her different boyfriends on different nights, and I washed the plates in warm water and stacked them by the sink. "A really good girl," she called me.

She tucked me into bed, and she told me bedtime stories. "There was the keeper of the donor list," she said. "There was the shredder of the master list. There was the marketing and the fundraising and also the development. There was late for work, and there was early. There was even right on time. The box of stamps and the corkboard calendar and the pink book of message sheets to tell you what happened exactly, specifically, in detail, While You Were Out."

She said the last four words in syncopation while taking

exaggerated steps backward from my bed, through the door, and down the hall, turning away. She left the door open a crack so a slice of light slipped across my face while I slept.

My mother and her boyfriends played cards late into the night, different games, different boyfriends for different nights of the week, their open arms spreading toward Sunday like a royal flush. I loved the way their voices carried up and over and into my unpillowed ear. Safe laughter, safe sleep. When it got too quiet, I drifted off, then startled myself awake, searching for their sounds, for proof of their happiness, like breath against a mirror.

In the mornings, I put the cards away and made coffee, stacked the pillows on the couch in the manner my mother liked them, two small pillows propped against a large decorative rectangle stitched with an old-fashioned phrase in elegant, swirly letters: *There Is Nothing More Personal Than Doing Your Job.*

My mother's pilot boyfriend promised us tickets around the world, but he only ever took us around the block. "It doesn't count if you make airplane arms," she said, sauntering behind us as we sailed down the street. My mother's cobbler boyfriend spiffed her shoes, then spiffed mine. My mother's tallest boyfriend was only five foot seven, but he lifted me onto his shoulders all the same, spun me through the living room in circles, and I feared my head would knock the ceiling.

"There used to be a taller boyfriend, but now this one's the tallest," my mother said. "Before he was the tallest, he was a baker."

Her baker still brought us fresh, warm baguettes every day, despite his new tall title.

"What happened to the very tallest boyfriend?" I asked.

"He's gone," she said, and she looked away, so I knew the subject was closed for business.

The academic boyfriend was my best friend. He presented me with stacks of books, leather bound and paper flapped, and we read them together, stretched out on the rug. He taught me about pirates, about buried treasure, about multiplication. He moved away to teach at a university. I cried into various fabrics, into blankets, into pillows, into scarves, and when I couldn't find any more fabrics, I cried into my mother's skirt. I slipped my hand into her pocket and stole her inky pens.

"Sometimes boyfriends leave," my mother said. "Your grandmother's boyfriends were all drafted into the same battalion. Every last one left, not one left over." She spun a glass between her hands like a potter at a wheel. "And your great-grandmother," she said, "had girlfriends."

Sundays we went to the park. My mother's beatnik boyfriend played bongos under a tree. Weekends with her hippie boyfriend, assembling crowns of thistle and dandelion for my brow. The street vendor boyfriend always made sure to save us something salty and, for later, something sweet. A pretzel, perhaps, followed by a bag of honeyed cashews. The pilot told stories about air travel, seat belts, small bottles of liquor (*this* small!), the space between the plane and the earth (*this* big!). Long distances. We would lay splat, flat on our backs and watch the jets like toys overhead, tiny novelties tinkering with a distance as bold as the sky.

"I'm going to marry the International Space Station," I said.

And my mother said, "Not us. That's not what we do." She meant the part about getting married.

Some days, our home was full to bursting. Three people: six arms, six legs, thirty toes, infinite hairs, infinite pores, infinite dreams. But I also liked the quiet days, just my mother and me. I liked when the boyfriends took a break. "We're taking a break," my mother would say, unprompted and unanswered. I liked when my mother had ideas about eating at the coffee table. Us, sitting at the dining table, and she would pick up her plate and walk across the room. I would pick up my plate and follow her. We would put our plates on the coffee table and pull it closer, close enough to touch our knees. There was a little shelf below the table, a kind of undertable, and that was where we placed our tall, cool drinks. This was the way we ate dinner, just the two of us, creating rings of condensation, wet little galaxies where there had been none.

"Much better," my mother said.

On warm nights, she kept the windows open, and bright leaves danced through the kitchen. Sometimes we cleaned the plates but forgot our drinks, hidden as they were under the table. Cups accumulated for days.

Just us. The dining table, vacated, was where we put our stuff. I stacked my paper-flapped books in the far corner. I wrote and drew with inky pens in my reserved spot, with my legs tucked up and crossed over the seat. In the colder half of autumn, I would hang my coat on the back of the cobbler's chair, and in the winter, I'd hang my scarf there too. Mom put her purse on the back of the beatnik's chair, and she strung the garbage bag on the back of another. We didn't use the trash bin during times like these. We didn't even mop or sweep. Chores disappeared into the vacuum, and we never vacuumed the three hundred square feet shared by us and only us. We took a large garbage bag and tied one flap to the arm of the pilot's chair. When it was full, almost too full to carry, we dragged it down the stairs and out onto the street.

Just us on Saturdays, and we didn't get dressed. We stayed in our sleepwear until it was time to go back to sleep. The windowsills were thick with slices of snow and ice, and I imagined our building as a tiny ship wedged in an ocean that had frozen solid, turned to land. Then the bustle renewed, the melting snow and the noise and the space filled with bodies, with people, with a boyfriend sitting at the table, with another boyfriend on the phone, with lives together and separate from our own, waxing and waning and crossing and connecting and swerving and departing. And then the chores returned, and the tasks, and the work of living in the world.

My mother was filling in for the Statue of Liberty. My mother was filling in for Lady Justice at the courthouse. My mother was filling in for the Mayor, and she stumped for the rights of temporaries across the boroughs. My mother was filling in for her mother. My mother was filling in for her mother's mother. For her mother's mother's mother. My mother was checking facts, and what she found was mostly poetry. My mother was filling in for the Funicular. She stretched herself from mountain to shore, stretched her skirt into a bindle to carry a skirtload of tourists, or so she said.

What I mean to say is that my mother was larger than life. My mother was very tired at the end of the day, when she turned out my lights and told me stories.

"And the pink book of messages explaining what happened exactly, specifically, While You Were Out."

She stepped backward and away and pulled the door until it clicked behind her, no seam of light lingering along the edge.

She took me away to start my jobs.

Events cluttered calendars, then got crossed off.

Events cluttered my leather-bound planner, but events were never annual.

My leather-bound planner fit in a leather bag I bought with my first paycheck. I strapped the bag across my chest like a song, and grabbed it with two hands where it belted my lungs.

One weekend, while visiting my mother, I found the academic boyfriend sitting on the rug reading a periodical. He had returned at last, without tenure. He was complaining to my mother about tenure. "Tenure!" he said. I was complaining about the world, about which I had brand new ideas, ideas that were brand new only to me. It was very important that I acted unimpressed. It was very important that I found his ideas particularly unfascinating. It was important, of course, that I seemed fascinating. I loosened my gait and looked anywhere but his face, his books, my dear old friend.

"I have ideas about the world!" I said.

"Tell me!" he said.

"You wouldn't understand," I said, and I went to my room and shut the door. I fell asleep on top of my blanket. When I woke up forty minutes later, spit dried on my cheek, the tenure of his visit had ended. He had left me a new stack of books.

I bought a futon for my new apartment and carried it upstairs. I met my very first boyfriend, my favorite boyfriend. He was at the grocery store in a halo of fluorescent light, pushing a cart full of foods that indicated an intermediate ability in the kitchen. He swiped his items for purchase against the self-serve register, and the register produced a series of beeps in affirmation, validation, a little song of beeps, some music for our meeting, some Morse code for warning. We carried our groceries side by side until I had traveled all the way to his place instead of mine.

Another weekend of visiting my mother, and we were trying to secure her benefits. She asked her employer for benefits, but the benefits went to the person she was temporarily replacing. My mother was replacing a skyscraper.

"Like, a building?" I asked, skeptical.

"You used to believe I could do anything," she said.

My mother was replacing the person who operated the elevators in the skyscraper. She deserved a single, shiny benefit.

"It would benefit us both," she wrote to her employer, at my suggestion. Her cobbler had made her a pair of shoes for the job. They sparkled like a skyline, but my mother's feet were useless all the same. The shoes she filled were constantly switching in size. Just imagine what that does to your feet.

Her employer sent her a plan for benefits, brand new benefits, a gleaming set of benefits, set to start at the end of her placement.

"Next time," he said.

"Next life," my mother said.

My mother had stopped hoping for steadiness long ago.

When the pilot boyfriend's plane went missing, we pretended it wasn't so. We stood on the skyscrapers my mother had temporarily replaced. We looked up. We looked for him. We were thankful for our tickets around the world, the tickets that never arrived, that could still exist in our imagination. We were thankful for the dream of the trip, which no doubt exceeded any trip we could've taken. We were thankful for the memory of his arms like the wings of a plane, swooping down our block in a single, sturdy line of flight.

I cancelled an interview with Farren. I cancelled a job grooming the canopy of a forest. I cancelled my marriage to the International Space Station.

One night, I accidentally left my leather bag on the train, and in the bag I left my leather planner. Gone. I bought a new planner at the planner store. The leather was stiff and sad and still smelled too much of animal.

I cut a weekend with my boyfriends short.

A weekend of visiting my mother, and she was feeling just OK. I put her in a spot of sunshine by the window, and she leaned into the warmth like a plant.

A weekend of visiting my mother, and I wanted to ask her

advice. My newest job involved a woman and a closet full of shoes.

"So many shoes," she said, impressed.

"I guess it's because she's lonely."

"Nothing more personal than that," she said, falling asleep against the arm of the couch.

My boyfriends multiplied by twos and threes, a response to forthcoming pain, perhaps, a bracing for an injury. We went on dates to our favorite bar, and I was happy. I could be happy and sad. It's the way I can multitask, it's the way two feelings can be the same feeling. It's the way a rash and a willow can both weep.

A weekend of visiting my mother, and she was very sick. The hospital room was crowded. Hands, legs, fingers, hairs, infinite pores, infinite dreams, infinite worlds, infinite tubes. I saw the beatnik, now more of a yuppie. I saw the hippie, now more of a hipster. I could see the boyfriends' many faces buried under current, somber faces. The street vendor went to the vending machine and brought me an ice-cold soda. The baker put a warm hand on my back. I remembered sitting on his shoulders as a child; now, his shoulders hunched, his nose measured just above my chin.

The very tallest boyfriend had also returned. I knew him only by his height, having never met him. Towering over the rest of us, slender and in a suit, like a crane in formal wear, leaning down next to the hospital bed, the better to do construction on my mother's health. When he was there, she laughed and spoke in her biggest voice. He hovered over the other boyfriends and covered her hand with his, a tarp for her tubes and needles. She seemed as if she were getting better. His head hit the ceiling when he walked through the door.

When a temp dies before the steadiness, it's said she's doomed to perform administrative work for the gods in perpetuity.

Weekends visiting my mother at her grave, I lay splat, flat on my back. I sometimes bring a picnic. I always go alone. I sometimes write things down. To tell her what happens exactly, specifically, in detail, While She Is Out.

Sky Work

The Agency for Fugitive Temps. Engaged when necessary to assist in damage control. Temps gone astray and jobs gone awry. With office outposts around the world, the AFT handles the paperwork, the protocol, the swishy cleanup of dark matters, derelict deeds, criminal materials. I take my place on the conveyor belt, at the back of the line for delinquent temps. All of us are carried along through a series of AFT interviews and questionnaires, fingerprinting and background checking, the belt delivering us past windows for stamping forms, cubbies for additional form distribution, and slots for the forms' eventual deposit.

"And who is your standard agency contact?" the clerk asks me.

"Farren," I say.

"They're all Farrens! Which one is yours?"

"Farren, comma, City."

"City Farren. Right. And who's your family contact?"

"Also Farren?"

"And who's your emergency contact?"

"I don't know. Farren, I guess?"

"Oh, I see, I see." The clerk murmurs something to another clerk, then they murmur in harmony. "And you were employed by a client named . . . Carl?"

"Yes, that's right."

"Oh gosh, don't you just love that guy?"

"I guess."

"But don't you just really love him? Like, *real soulmate* love?"

"Maybe. Maybe I really did love him." It hurts to think about it, but think about it I must. It's part of the questionnaire.

"But not *too* much, right? Like real, nonsexy, soulmate love? Like he was your soulmate employer?"

"Is that a thing?"

"Oh, you! You're funny." The clerk laughs so hard she snorts. "Anyway. Eh. Nee. Way. Such a great boss, that Carl. We hear such great things! Such a shame about the whole *prison* situation, right?" the clerk asks with a conspiratorial tilt of the head.

"A real shame." I look around and wonder, Are these other temps in quite as much trouble as I am? Or maybe their trouble is worse.

The conveyor belt dumps us in a waiting room where we sit and stew over our forthcoming placements.

"Temp Number Five! Number Five, come to the front for your placement!"

"Temp Number Fourteen! Oh no, I'm sorry. Temp Number Fifteen! Come to the front and bring your ticket."

"The idea," Temp Fourteen says with a nasal whisper, "is to keep us hidden, keep us repentant." She reclaims her seat, ticket clutched in her hand.

"Are any of the fugitive placements desirable?" I ask.

"Oh no," she says, conferring with some of the other women, dealing out sticks of gum like aces and queens. "But they're a necessary beat on the path back to the steadiness. This is my third time through the AFT."

This temp is twice my age, and her feet are now resting, elevated on a stool. She massages her ankles and curses the whole system. She's been on this road long enough to know she should've already arrived. "When can a woman get a break?" this temp asks. No one answers. She waits for someone to answer; it wasn't rhetorical. But we just chew our gum and look away. Long after my number is called, I imagine she waits there still.

I report for work at the designated location and am met by a blimp the size of the moon, hovering in the sky and lowering a ladder.

"Climb on up!" an amplified voice calls down.

I climb the dangling ropes and take my position in the clouds.

Aboard the blimp, the fugitive temps push buttons. The supervisor tells us when to push which button and where, and how, but not why. I'm still in training, so daily I observe the process.

"Push the fourth button from the left," she says. "Push it twice, then hold it down a third time for twenty seconds. On my count."

After pushing buttons, we take our dinners and sleep on cots, all the while sailing through galaxies of birds, of stars. I understand this location, as hidden as humanly possible, authorities on the lookout and fugitives going right over their heads.

On my first day of training, I recognize the man pushing buttons at the end of the row of button pushers.

"Barnacle Toby?"

"Oh hey, it's you!" He gives me a big, unexpected hug and a punch to the shoulder. "You can call me Harold. After all, I'm not a barnacle anymore."

"Harold," I say, "what are you doing here?"

"Kicked out of the ocean for changing the emotional pH of my sector. My feelings were killing all the surrounding aquatic life. I have that effect on people, and apparently also on shrimp." Harold hands me a cup and fills it with coffee. "The AFT assigned me here about a month ago."

"It's so good to see a familiar face," I say, but I'm surprised I even recognize him without his strata of crabs and shells and seaweed. I'm surprised he recognizes me.

"Same to you, buddy! What brings you to this esteemed locale?"

"Oh, you know, a botched murder situation."

"Right, right, right. Well then, you'll fit in here perfectly."

"What does that mean?"

The supervisor walks by and Harold goes quiet. He waits until she's out of earshot. "Ah . . . You don't know what the buttons are for, do you?" he says.

"No, I didn't think anyone knew." Frankly, I was starting to wonder if the buttons did anything at all. It wouldn't be the first time I'd worked a job with no discernible impact.

Harold leans in close, so his mouth is nearly touching the edge of my ear. "Bombs," he whispers. "As in, dropping them."

Each combination of button maneuvers drops a bomb on a specified location. The sequences are verified and predetermined by the owners of the blimp. Harold thinks the owners are a conglomeration of allied countries, or a single evil billionaire, or a supervillain, or a real estate mogul bombing his own properties and making hay with the insurance money.

Harold explains that if the supervisor doesn't touch the buttons, then technically, she doesn't drop the bombs. And if the supervisor doesn't drop the bombs, then neither does the owner of the blimp. And since fugitive temps are hidden and without recourse, we technically don't exist, at least not in the eyes of the law. And if no one drops the bombs, no one can be blamed for dropping the bombs, and no one can be tried, and no one can be hanged, and no one can be held accountable, and it's maybe as if the bombs were released by none other than the wide and wondrous sky itself.

On his cot, Harold gets philosophical. "You know what they don't tell you about being a barnacle?" he asks, unprompted.

"What's that?"

"They don't tell you that you never stop feeling like a barnacle, not really. Sure, you can walk and run and jump again. You can give your fellow temp a hug or a cup of coffee. You can climb aboard a zeppelin. Your dick can even return to its normal, totally average size. But that saltwater kick is still in your veins. It doesn't go away."

I wonder if it's still in my veins too. If I summon it, could I feel the ocean in an instant? Am I still a pirate, somewhere deep? Am I still a mannequin? Am I still a girl pretending to be a ghost? Thank goodness I'm sitting down, because the feelings rush over me like a large, violent wave, and for a moment I lose my balance and can't breathe. Then I remember what Harold told me about his feelings, their way of changing the pH, expanding, infiltrating. Hurting.

The next morning, one of our colleagues refuses to press her buttons.

"What do you mean, refuse?" the supervisor asks.

"I refuse," the temp says again.

"Refuse how?"

"I refuse vehemently."

Harold gives me a look, mouths *uh-oh*.

"Vehemently?" the supervisor repeats, eyes bulging.

"At the very most, I refuse vehemently. At the very least, I refuse firmly. Firmly like a good mattress."

"And on what grounds?"

"Which grounds where?"

"On what grounds do you refuse firmly, like a good mattress?"

"Not on grounds, on clouds."

"What kind of clouds?"

"Moral ones," our colleague says. "I refuse on moral clouds."

"This is preposterous," the supervisor says. She's pacing around the blimp, arms clasped behind her back. "I've never heard of such a thing—morals!"

"Well, life is full of firsts."

"You know the consequence of insubordination, don't you?"

"I do," our coworker says, her feet firmly planted.

Would my feet be as firm as hers, or even as firm as a good mattress? I haven't been instructed to press a single button yet, not until I complete my training. What kind of buttons will these buttons press inside me?

"Very well," the supervisor says. She opens a hatch and shoves our colleague out into the moral clouds. "What a waste of a morning!" the supervisor says, wiping her hands and shaking her head, walking to her office. She turns back one last time. "Harold, will you take over for the unmanned buttons?"

Harold nods and sinks into his chair. With a combination of several jabs, he releases a bomb on who knows where, what, whom.

"Don't look at me like that," he says, but no one is looking at him. We're all looking at the hatch, now closed, pondering its hatch-like capabilities with our mouths hanging open, unhatched.

I think about the fallen temp, dropping like a bomb herself, and it gives me an idea, a sort of dirigible plan that will burst if I'm not careful.

My necklace burns around my neck.

"Something brewing, eh?" the Chairman says, perched on the edge of my cot, pistachios in hand.

"Always," I say, happy to see a familiar face.

"I never thought I'd make it to heaven, but this sure is close!" he says, peering out the zeppelin's window. "Who's a man about town now? More like a man above town!"

I ask the Chairman of the Board, "If you wanted to find a series of codes, codes for, say, dropping bombs, where would you look?"

"Where would I look?" he says, and in an instant, he's gone. It's as if the answer to my question has climbed from my necklace and into my head.

When everyone on board is asleep, I rummage through the supervisor's desk and find her own leather-bound planner. It looks just like mine. Is the supervisor a temp too? In the planner, there are button combinations for every location in the city, in the sea, in the world, beyond. Longitudes and latitudes for everything I love.

The trick is to hit the prison at just the right angle, so as not to injure the inmates or the guards. If I pick the right location in the vicinity as opposed to straight on, I can allow for their escape. A little bit of freedom. For Carl.

It's the fifth button, and then a hold on the seventeenth button to a count of nine, then three short punches on button number six.

It takes more time to press the buttons than it does for the alarms to sound.

"What were you thinking?" Harold asks, pulling me away from the buttons. "You know the consequence for insubordination!"

"Harold, subordination doesn't lead to the steadiness." As soon as I say it, I know it's true. A lump rises in my throat, and I'm overcome with emotion. "I want to feel my feet on the ground, forever. I want to be a standard human person with a place to belong. How can I ever become permanent if I don't travel through some moral clouds?"

Harold smiles. "There's the barnacle I used to know," he says, but I haven't the faintest idea what kind of barnacle I used to be, or what kind of barnacle I've become. What does he know about me? What does anyone know? That's the point.

"You," the supervisor says, running toward us. "What were you thinking?"

"I was just thinking differently."

"Who said you get to think differently?"

"No one."

"And who is this no one?"

"Not anyone. Not you."

"That's right," she seethes. "I didn't say anything about thinking. I didn't say anything at all! How does this all work, without me? Without *me*!" the supervisor yells.

The other fugitive temps sit silently at their button stations.

"You think you can hit just any old button, whenever you want?" She slams her palm down on several buttons at a time as a demonstration, dropping bombs all over.

"Is that absolutely necessary?" Harold asks, barely audible.

"Oh, it's necessary. It's necessary. I'm proving a point!"

The supervisor is losing control. She shoves Harold out of the way and heads straight for me.

"Thank you for the opportunity," I say, "but it's time to submit my notice."

I unlock the hatch.

I remember the plank.

I remember how to fall, and so, I jump.

The clouds, one by one, lift toward me and race away, as though the sky moves while I stay perfectly still. Faster and faster into the air, I feel the world rushing ahead, speeding into motion, deadly as concrete.

The Chairman was smart to suggest a parachute, and when the moment arrives, I pull it and it blossoms.

Now I float easily, carried by the wind. In the distance, rubble everywhere. The supervisor's tantrum has released bombs here and there, all over. There, the murder shack, gone. There, the bank, blown to smithereens. The safe looks so tiny from this height, like a toy, sprung loose and unlocked. I make out the smallest figurine version of Laurette, masked and ready, loading sacks of money into larger sacks.

"Laurette!" I yell.

Maybe it's the altitude, the lack of oxygen, but Laurette sees me and waves. "Oh, honey! Where will you go now?" she calls.

"I never know!" I say.

Laurette nods with a deep swing of chin to chest. I'm a double fugitive, a fugitive twice removed. "Good luck to you forever!" she says, and she waves with her whole arm, finger to shoulder.

I fall in parallel to buildings as high as the sky. Through the windows, people looking out windows, looking at me, looking at the decimation of the city. Through the windows, other windows, doorways flanked with office plants and leather furniture. Boardrooms, boardrooms, boardrooms.

There, the prison—I've hit my mark. The gates are thrown open, prisoners running out and through the forest, over the bridge, into town. I see Carl's buddy, running for the hills. I see Carl, standing near the fractured fence, his eyes brimming with recognition. Again, the altitude.

"Hey buddy!" I yell in Carl's direction.

He doesn't respond. Am I talking to myself? I'm still awfully high up.

"Hey buddy!" I say again.

"You're not my buddy," he says. "You're no buddy of mine."

"Carl! I did this for you! This loving, solitary thing!"

"Solitary? What do you know about solitary? You left me here to rot in solitary."

The closer the parachute brings me to Carl, the farther

away he seems. I can't help but feel angry with him and the way he shows his appreciation for my hard work, my dedication. I'm shocked to realize I expected more, more than what I was promised, more than something short term. I feel silly for expecting anything at all.

"We're better at doing time," I say, "when we do it together."

Carl looks at me once more, then runs off with the other prisoners. He doesn't look back.

I see them race forward together, trailing through the city, fugitives, all of us.

My parachute hovers over a hole in the ground, perhaps the bomb's crater, and I allow the drop to continue down, my heart still broken, down, I hope, to the center of the earth. The flower of the parachute deflates and leaves me stuck at the bottom of the hole, which opens into a hidden tunnel.

I scramble like a rodent, elbows greased with mud. The tunnel widens and shrinks and widens and squeezes and widens to reveal strings of lights, brightening the path.

I crawl.

I've gone from cloud dweller to subterranean creature.

The tunnel is soft, wet. The pulp of the earth seeps under my nails. Does earth under a nail make the nail a claw? And then a rockier passage, then I journey to the right and the mud changes, sewage puddles under knees, the grout of swirling oils and fibers, measureless caverns, a different trail of knee marks, of claw marks, a different smell, no, a stench, and I understand, of course, this is a detour, a false tunnel, a carpal tunnel, a corporeal tunnel, not the true tunnel, probably a dead end, and what will I do, where will I go, how will I survive, especially if the lights go out?

The lights go out.

In the perfect darkness I feel calm, maybe even happy. I feel the floating joy of a world without walls, without bodies, without days, without a single worldly thing. I feel my face and I don't know how it's positioned in relation to the sun. This lack of perspective somehow makes me hopeful. I'm a seed unsprouted. I think I even smile. I think I even sleep.

Time moves and then does not move. The darkness schedules an illusion of motion, an illusion of stopping, could be backward, could be forward, timecards punching and unpunching. Time travel is my newest skill, in the wormhole with the mud and the muck and the worms, the silent, earthen company I keep.

I think I even sleep, then I go ahead and sleep some more.

It might be minutes, months.

From just above my head, or perhaps from just below, a hand pulls at my collar and yanks until my knees respond, my cramped joints unravel, and I see that I can stand up perfectly straight. A clearing. I shake off the animal I've become and roll my spine until I'm walking tall, shuffling with half steps. The hand adjusts my shoulders, lifts my wrist to grab a ladder, and, holding mostly steady, with a bit of guidance, I raise my leg and my chin. I climb into the cave of the witch.

Paper Work

"Not a witch, per se," she says. "I prefer Director of Pamphlets."

She hands me a business card, and then, "Here, have an extra."

She's young for a director, and frazzled, and generous with laughter, and her hair shines like a wave of charitable donations.

She hands me a stack of pamphlets to peruse. It's painful to look at them, and they sting to the touch. Fine little nicks in the flesh of my fingers, and I think, Do they have teeth? Are they enchanted?

"It hurts," I say.

"The pamphlets are also hurting," she says, stroking one with a coarse, knobby thumb. "We hurt each other. We need each other." Her nose is as slim and straight as a bone-folded binding.

"I'm looking for a new placement," I say, furious with myself. Even without Farren, I flee from job to job. The steadiness evades me, and I can't help myself. When I see a job, it needs taking.

"I sure could use an extra set of hands," she says. "These days, we have a lot of information to disseminate. Killers on the loose. Bombs in the skies. Dangerous times!"

The cave is damp and cold, and she is alone here, the Director of Pamphlets, with her pamphlets on her desk and the algae on the walls molding dank and dark and hostile, and I picture her lungs full of the same variety of vicious growth. I feel her loneliness like a stalactite stuck to the roof of my mouth. She folds new pamphlets of magenta and chartreuse, her fingers covered in cuts and burns.

"Where are we?" I ask.

"This is the corridor for the alchemy of company literature."

She leads me to the entrance of the cave and points down the street. It looks like a normal street.

"Door to door," she says. "You know the drill, don't you? Here's your uniform."

She drapes me in a nonprofit poncho full of pockets, to carry the many pamphlets. She smiles.

"Won't you join me on my first day?" I ask, assuming I need some supervision.

"No," she laughs. "I can't leave!"

"Oh, I'm sorry."

"Don't let me leave," she gasps, suddenly grabbing my arm. "And don't come back," she says, "until every pamphlet has a home."

"Every pamphlet?"

"It's essential," she says, "that every pamphlet is distributed. If you don't distribute every pamphlet, bad things happen."

"What kinds of bad things?"

"Oh, that's not important!" Away and into the world with a placement I placed for myself.

Here I am, the knocker of doors. Here I am, the distributor of pamphlets. Do you recognize this man? Do you know how to stay safe in the event of an attack? Have you seen something, or said anything?

"It doesn't matter what you offer," the Director of Pamphlets says, laughing. "It doesn't matter what you say, as long as they take a pamphlet."

Here I am, here to knock on your door. Please take a pamphlet, and please that's all. The Director says I should always say please. "It increases the chances of pamphlet distribution, tenfold," she says.

Please can I trouble you for a moment of your time, folded as it is, compressed as your weeks are, like a pamphlet of weeks? Can I tell you a bit about what we do? Can I tell you a noise complaint from next door? Can I tell you your future? In your future, you'll hold a pamphlet. Can I fold the pamphlet into an accordion and play you a song? Can I fold it into a fan and fan your face? Can I put it in your pocket when you aren't looking, then put your pocket in the wash, dampen the pamphlet into grainy mulch, then reconstitute the pamphlet with a set of tweezers? Do you want to buy some cookies? Well, don't we all.

First, how many people live in your home, and would you like to support our cause? Will you buy some citrus fruit? Will you study our research? Will you consider the numbers? Will you continue to ignore the facts? When will you take a stand? Why don't you take a seat? Would you care for some literature?

Here I am, here to please, to knock on your heart, tug on your sleeve, and sir, do you have a moment to discuss your life goals? The state of the economy? The state that wants secession? The recession of hair, of tides? The ceasefire and the forest fire and the brand-new flavor of fire-roasted pretzels? The exegesis of today's front-page headlines? The story of how the world will end, slash, how the world began, slash, what kind of world is this, anyway, slash, how 'bout that certain team that plays that certain sport? How about the environment? The economy? The bathroom? As in, can I use yours? Do you like comedy?

Would you perhaps consider a list of vintage novelties you played with as a child? A listicle of popsicles you ate as a child? The story of your inner child? The story of the baby and the bathwater? The story of the baby otter and the baby giraffe and their unlikely friendship?

"Can you just skip the stories and give me the pamphlet?" one man says. I give him a pamphlet gladly, and he places it on a pile of other pamphlets from other companies, on the handy pamphlet table in his home's entryway, an aedicula to life's mysterious accumulation of printed collateral.

"For pamphlets," he says, pointing to the table. "For scraps." He points again. "For ephemera."

I stand on a corner and supply pamphlets, a steady stream of paper, the reflexive pedestrians and their involuntary grabs, clasping the pamphlets and walking forward, their hands turning red with rashes from the pamphlets, and from above, an aerial, blimplike view of pamphlets scattering and spreading through the streets, a sharp confetti cutting the city with wonder.

I return to the cave pamphlet-free.

"I'm impressed," says the Director, pouring me drink. "Cocktails!"

Her cheeks are a field of freckles, fine lines of smiles, and she pays me with a wad of cash.

"We'd also like to give you the very special opportunity to donate a portion of your payment to the further creation of pamphlets."

I oblige.

More pamphlets in the morning, but first, the Director reminds me to distribute every single pamphlet. "We can't risk any stray pamphlets making their way back to this cave."

Then door to door and down the sidewalk, around the block and across the city, with my poncho full of pamphlets. A thin drizzle dissecting the day. Around the cul-de-sacs and the one-way streets and the small-jointed streets and the bony ligamenture of corner stores connecting a skeleton of avenues. A pamphlet for the man who makes the artisan paninis.

Can I interest you in a pamphlet about your rights? Can I interest you in a pamphlet about my rights? How about restrictions? Directions? Can I offer you a pamphlet with pictures of your body, to tell you about your body, an instruction manual for how your body works, as told to you by someone else?

Please ma'am, have a pamphlet. Take it in your hand and pull it through your door and put it away. Forget about it for a year, then remember and find it in a folder full of take-out menus and old to-do lists. Struggle to read the pamphlet and struggle to touch the pamphlet. "Ouch!" you'll say. "I can't deal with this right now!" you'll say. "It hurts in a way I can't describe!" Put the pamphlet back into the folder, put the folder away, and label the folder IMPORTANT, then repeat those steps year after year, new haircut, new house, new husband, new haircut, new car, new husband, until the pamphlet softens with creases and pressure from piles of pamphlets, piles of tasks nearly complete, in a box of documents for sorting, a box of documents for shredding. Then finally shred the pamphlet, because you can't throw the pamphlet away, not ever, because you throw away only things that are useless. And though you're not certain of the pamphlet's use, you know the pamphlet is useful. You know it's important. You've felt it working on your life, a silent sacred work, a life guided by possession of the pamphlet. And though you're not sure why, you know you've been changed by the presence of this slip of paper, this slip that somehow hurts, that cuts, that has no use except to remind you of something (what?), of someplace (where?), of your first husband sitting on the porch the day the pamphlet first fell into your hands. No use except to convince you, over and over, that you'll probably need it, probably use it, probably redeem it, probably redeem yourself, someday.

"Can I have two?" the woman asks.

"No," I say.

I return to the cave pamphlet-free, my fingers swollen with welts.

"Great work," says the Director of Pamphlets.

There is certain work that cannot be done well and cannot be done poorly. It can only be done or undone. There is no success metric for a job that simply keeps me busy, so I ignore her empty praise.

She asks, "Are you game for a night shift?"

"Of course," I say, and I travel up and down the streets, distributing pamphlets with pictures of Carl's face emblazoned in thick, drippy ink. Fugitive, the pamphlet says.

I return to the cave wearing my empty-pocket poncho, whistling a pamphlet-placing tune. The Director is crying, and her cave swallows the sobs, releases them as growls. In certain kinds of light, the waves in her hair resemble scales.

"Thank god you're back," she says, the growls subsiding, her curls unfurling in a waterfall over her shoulders, not a scale to be seen. "My pamphlets! My poor pamphlets," she says, "alone out there in the world."

"Is that not where they're meant to be?"

"There's been a clerical error," she says. "We printed the wrong kind. The wrong color! The wrong font! With typos, no less."

"I see," I say, and I hang my poncho near the entrance of the cave.

"You need to retrieve all the pamphlets, every last one."

"Just take them back?"

"Take them back," she coughs, wiping her nose. "Remember, it's the same rules. If you don't retrieve every single pamphlet, bad things will happen. Oh, my poor pamphlets!"

I shrug the poncho over my shoulders and turn around to retrace my steps. Please, can I retrieve this pamphlet? Please can I take it back to my cave? Some stops are luckier than others. One woman has already put her pamphlet in the recycling, and I find it crushed in the bin next to her front door.

A man finds a pamphlet stuck under his welcome mat. "Ow," he says, tossing it into my hands like something scalding hot.

A woman is using her pamphlet as a placemat. "Ouch," she says, flicking it at my face like something frozen.

"Here," a family says, removing a magnet from their fridge with a tough team effort and sliding the pamphlet into my open pocket.

If I distribute a pamphlet, then repossess the same pamphlet, is the entire experience erased? What should I do with the elegance of this revision, a revision that also erases me? I decide to leave some small remainder in the world, some unretrieved pamphlets, unsought. I know that I've been warned against this course of action, but I can't bear the task that makes and unmakes. Because in the end, what does that make of me?

I return to the cave with pockets full of pamphlets, not all, but many. The Director of Pamphlets stands at work against the moldy walls, and she doesn't see me enter. But I see her clearly. She has a tail and wisps of leathery flesh framing her face. The smile lines are now growl lines, deep valleys unveiled around her mouth, unleashing a wave of flame. Or no, something like flame, something adjacent, not exactly flame, but a glamorous sort of blue heat, flecks of gold, odd and gleaming and flowing from the Director's mouth and into a pile of newly folded pamphlets.

"Um," I manage to say.

She turns toward me and reveals her face, wizened like a wet, organic root, something for smoothies, something, honestly, beautiful.

"What?" she roars, handing me the new stack of pamphlets, fresh from printing. "Here. Typo's fixed. I corrected them while you were out."

"Right. And did anything else happen . . . while I was out?"

It takes her a minute to notice her scales, her tail, the length of it curling up and around her face, her eyes growing wide at the sight. "I see you didn't retrieve the full stack," she says, her voice growing deeper and more reptilian by the minute.

"I retrieved most of them!"

"I told you," she says, a snarl encroaching on her mouth, revealing a tooth the size of my hand, "that bad things would happen."

The Director lifts herself onto her haunches and sprouts wings from her back. She flies out of the cave and into the world. I've released her, which was not something I was supposed to do.

I pocket the pamphlets and pocket my possessions.

The time I spend now is time spent with pamphlets. I think, if I continue to distribute them, I might just rein my employer back into her cave. I try a street I haven't tried yet, and I pamphlet the street with pride. I turn down another street, giving in to the laziness of mailboxes, mail slots, setting a pamphlet in the cuticle of a glass-framed door. I ring a couple of bells now and then, but the solitude isn't horrible. I notice a nodule of boredom hiding in my mind, and I want to pick it. I pick it until it bleeds. Other times, boredom blossoms in my chest like a lush chord, an empty schedule, the luxury of freshly fallen snow. The boredom of the pamphlets canvasses my expectations, papering my peripatetic life into a single, boring document that makes a kind of folded sense.

The next street looks familiar. I stand in the center of the road and feel another version of myself, standing in the same spot. Have I been here before? I carry my pamphlets to the door of a house down the way, a lovely little house, hydrangea bushes framing the entrance, windows luminescent. A woman wearing a glorious gold watch answers my knocking, her bangs clipped from her forehead with a tiny silver pin.

Anna.

Anna's home, an elegant tree house of warm smells and subtle touches. High polish on the floors. A miniature mirror winking above a kitchen cabinet. A tapestry pinched into a playful tent, hovering over an overstuffed chair in the corner. Bright, crisp notes from the chimes outside her window, calculating the arithmetic of evening winds with their song. Hints of lemon and grease and honey, boiling liquids and roasted root vegetables, covered, then later, uncovered, browned, crisped, burned by accident, scraped and replaced with brand-new turnips and radishes and sprouts, no problem, squat and fat and fresh from the fridge. Heirloom tomatoes on the cutting board and heirloom treasures on the mantle. The entire scene shines like the contents of an animated sparkle on the edge of some glinting, watery eye. She holds me in her cashmere arms and hugs me to her chest, all the way into her nest, uses the hug as a pulley to reel me into her house.

"This house," says Anna, cashmere arms open wide. "My house. I own this house."

My entire face is trembling, and there is little I can do to stop it. Oh, Anna, is what I mean to say.

"Do you want a pamphlet?" is all I can manage.

She looks bewildered.

"Yes, of course," she says politely.

She reaches out, but I don't let her touch it with her hands, her little cream-tipped nails and her delicate rings and the gold watch that still fits her wrist after all these years.

"Here, for you," I say, and I put the pamphlet in her pamphlet basket near the door. She has baskets in every shape, stacked in every size, for just about every type of storage consideration. She looks at my filthy, stolen boots, and I understand I'm meant to remove them, place them in a basket. They slide off easily now, finally broken in.

"Can I fetch you a glass of water?" Anna asks. None of the things we used to do make sense anymore, but I guess we both still drink water. We drink some water side by side, our bodies full of fluids, of blood and acid and methods of hydration, caffeination, intoxication. Would I like to sit down, Anna wants to know. "Sure," I say, and now we're two women, formerly two girls, sitting down. I realize we've never before been under a roof, indoors, inside, together. Always sitting in the middle of the road, in a driveway, on a path, on pavement connected to streets, to highways, to interstates for which to someday travel.

"It's been a long, long time," Anna says.

"Has it?"

"Of course it has. But I'd recognize you anywhere."

"Same."

"That forehead!" she says, and I don't know what she means. She pauses for a sip of water, and the silence is excruciating. Then, "Are you here on vacation? Are you visiting someone special?"

"I'm looking for my next placement. What about you?"

"I live here," she says, gesturing to the room, confused. "Remember?"

"I mean, for your current placement."

"No. I don't do placements. I don't do that anymore."

"Oh?"

"I hopped from that old delivery truck to another delivery truck and to a bus and to a train across the country, and when I came back, I came back with the steadiness. A real job. A *dream* job!" She cups her chin in her hands and squeezes her eyes shut, a princess with a granted wish.

"A permanent job?"

"Yeah," and she sounds disappointed by my lack of excitement. "Like, you know, a regular job." She lobs the word *regular* in the manner of an eye roll.

I tuck my feet up onto the couch and under my thighs, but is that too informal? The holes in my socks are showing, and I slowly slide my feet back to the floor.

"What does it feel like?" I ask, trying not to cry. "The steadiness?"

"Oh, you know, it's hard to describe. Maybe like a rolling pin running over my shins? No, that's not right. Maybe like a Slinky wrapped around my hand? No, not that either. It's really different for everyone. Well, not everyone."

"Not everyone," I say, and it's like stretching open a sealed scar.

"I didn't mean it like that!" she cries. "Don't worry. When you know, you just know!"

I hope she won't say the next thing, but she says it anyway.

"Sometimes these things happen when you're not looking for them." Anna smiles.

"Where do you work?" I ask, trying to change the subject, barely breathing. "Where is your regular job?"

"At the bank," Anna says, wrapping herself in a cashmere throw. She is cashmere upon cashmere.

"Which one?"

"They make it so confusing," she says, "but between you and me, it's really all the same bank. Just one bank. All those robberies barely make a dent."

I can still picture Laurette slicing and shoving, locking the safe, blood pooling on the floor.

"Are you by any chance ever assigned to clean the bank?" I ask.

"Oh my god, you're so funny," Anna says, and she gulps her water like it's something stiffer. "I don't ever have to clean anything, not even my own house."

"Right."

"We need to treat ourselves kindly, you know!" Anna declares. "Especially right now, with all the bombings and the fugitives. And I heard something about a wild beast, like a dragon? What even *is* this life?" She shakes her head, then laughs. A real, happy laugh.

My whole body starts to shake, but am I sad? Am I cold? Am I safe? Am I scared?

"You're practically quaking!" Anna says, and she wraps me in the other end of her cashmere throw, really just a fringed corner. We sit like this for a moment, both comfortable and not, Anna's mouth curved into an expression I can't decipher. When we were younger, every door was a secret door. Every mollusk perhaps contained a pearl. We could anticipate rooms hidden behind other rooms, or meaty carcasses buried under mounds of soil. We wandered every surface with amazed suspicion. Now, Anna scoops up all the mystery for herself, tossing it over her shoulders like an oversized sweater. I surmise this much: Getting older is the difference between solving mysteries and studying to become one.

A round voice bounces down the stairs, inaudible but jolly. Anna has apparently understood the voice, because she yells, "Just a minute, babe!" Her posture changes, shoulders popping, head bobbing.

"We were about to watch a movie," she says, and for the first time I notice the two glasses, two plates. The pair of napkins. Two remote controls and two more on a shelf, and another remote in a ceramic dish.

"So many remotes."

"I know. We always lose track of which does what. I can never change the volume!" She tucks her feet up under her thighs, and I feel I've been invited to do the same. She leans into the couch with a long yawn, and I think, Is Anna bored?

"You should stay," Anna says with a pout, her eyes half closed. But the word *stay* has two syllables in her mouth—*stay-ee*—and I recognize that second syllable. It's the extra square foot, the exit where I'm supposed to see myself out.

"No, no, I really shouldn't."

"But wouldn't you like to join us? Wouldn't you like to *stay-ee*? You've only just arrived."

"I've seen this one already. On an enormous screen." I point at the television. The film is paused on a frame from the opening credits, which I recognize from the pirate captain's movie retrospective. "I've seen it big projector–style," I say.

"Fun! Like an outdoor movie in the park?"

"Yes, like an outdoor movie in the park."

"Cool. But we can watch something else. We can watch anything. Or nothing. *Stay-ee*!"

"OK. OK, maybe I will."

Satisfied, Anna tucks her cashmere sleeves into a cashmere cardigan under the cashmere blanket. Cashmere upon cashmere upon cashmere, a cocoon: She softens herself daily, in preparation for receiving love. Then she stretches out her arms and grabs me by the shoulders, reaching forward in parallel lines. At first I take it as a gesture of affection. But on further consideration, it's really an ambiguous pose, isn't it, the shoulder bridge, holding onto someone and also holding someone at bay, and she backs away into the kitchen, like a mammal running scared, to retrieve a board of cheese.

The round voice bouncing down the stairs once again. I think I hear the name Anna, or some variation on that theme.

"I need to go up to the bedroom for a second," she says, a cube of cheese on her tongue. "You're fine for a minute? It won't be long."

"Of course, Anna," I say.

"I can't believe you're really here," she says, and I know

the sentiment is genuine. She looks for a cheese knife on the counter. She opens a drawer next to the sink, then closes the drawer, then opens it again and closes it once more, opens it, closes it. She breathes out in a long, steady breath. "Old habits." She shrugs and opens the drawer one more time. She climbs the stairs in long strides.

I pause for a beat, then I collect my shoes and leave. A ghost again set free.

It's not for me, this kind of moment. Something inside me can't be contained by the shape of her house, her life. Something about me does not and will not fit. I feel myself protruding like a broken bone, breaking through the skin. Perhaps it's a matter of qualifications, the way they both certify and prohibit, the way I find the fullness of my life constantly halved, constantly qualified. Could I someday be qualified for happiness, for steadiness?

I wander the streets until crepuscular notions settle over the silent town, a single moonbeam gifting me my route back through the city.

The last time I see Anna, I see her in a dream. The last time you see someone is never the last time you see them. The empty space a person leaves behind retains heat; a retina will preserve a face for later. In the dream, Anna wanders toward me through a park, wearing a cashmere jumpsuit. Her eyes are fixed on mine, but as she approaches, I notice they're looking past, through, beyond. I notice it isn't even Anna at all.

"Anna?"

"Anna to you too," she says, and she continues walking.

"Do you know that girl?" the Chairman of the Board asks. My necklace burns even in sleep, and he strolls beside me.

"Not anymore," I say, and we link arms and leap into a conference call, holding steady on the line.

I hold the line for my favorite boyfriend, standing at a phone in the back of a bar on the other side of town. I remember the bar at home with longing, and the boyfriends, and their favorite drinks, none of which are on the menu here. I can't even start a tab properly in their honor. My favorite boyfriend devotes himself exclusively to pumpkin spice this time of year, in his cocktails and his coffee and his attitude. A one-man harvest for the coming cold.

"Hello?" he says. He sounds calm and distant.

"It's me," I say.

"Me?" he asks. Then, "Oh, right. Hi, you."

"Everything OK?"

"Better than OK," he says. "Hold on," and the phone spits out garbled sounds. "There. Now you're on speaker."

"Hi, everyone!" I say, but I'm met with a bothered silence, mumbles and half phrases.

"Should we invite her?" one voice whispers, perhaps my flaneur boyfriend, always concerning himself with the etiquette of breaking my heart.

"It would be the classy thing to do," my frugal boyfriend says, "if we can swing the cost."

"What's the protocol at the venue?" my real estate boyfriend wonders aloud.

"We haven't even voted on a venue!" another voice complains.

"Invite me where?" I ask. "Invite me to what?"

"To the wedding!" my earnest boyfriend says.

I hear the other boyfriends groan. "Way to spill the beans." "Nice going, buddy." "Just blurt it out, why don't you?"

"I'm sorry?"

"We're getting married," the tallest boyfriend says.

"All of you? All of you are getting married?"

"Not at the same time, but in the same lifetime," says the food systems analyst. "I'm baking the cake, obviously."

"Cakes, plural!" says my caffeinated boyfriend. "Ganache," he swoons. "Coffee."

"I don't understand."

"I'm getting married first," says my agnostic boyfriend.

"And I'm taking the two years after that," says the insurance salesman. "End of life is much too risky."

"Middle age!" shouts my gym rat boyfriend to cheers and wahoos and hollers of approval.

"I've been assigned *the separation*," says my handy boyfriend. "I can fix anything, even a marriage."

"But who? But who are you marrying?"

From the back of my apartment—because I know they're standing, lounging, hanging, as usual, at my apartment, at the Hangout—from within the invading force of boyfriends, I can detect a kernel of static. No, laughter. Gentle hiccups. Champagne popping? A soft tap of fingernails on a table, a giggle, and the noises surrounding a smile.

"Hi, superstar," says Farren. Her voice hits me in the head and nearly knocks me down.

"Farren?"

"Don't sound so surprised. As we say at the agency, You cruise, you lose. By the way," she adds, "I love your pet lizard!"

"When you didn't come back," says my favorite boyfriend, "we asked Farren to find us a replacement."

"They didn't have to look far. This is a placement I feel fit to cover!" Farren says, and I hear the boyfriends laugh with her. I laugh too, a reflex, because I feel utterly banished. I cough the laugh into my hand, disgusted. So devastated it might as well be a scream. The boyfriends are a swirling pool of sound, and I can no longer distinguish their voices.

"We're going to be *husbands*!" they cheer.

"And maybe then we'll be *fathers*!"

"And I'm going to be *you*!" Farren says. Good old Farren, faring so very well for herself, fare thee well to me.

They explain that after much deliberation, Farren voted my life coach boyfriend out of the apartment. He was having problems with the other boyfriends, real problems manifested in encounters, confrontations, microaggressions, the hijacking of date nights, and if you can't get along with your housemates, you can't get along with your life mate, or so the saying goes.

"Farren is a superb mediator," says my pacifist boyfriend. "Superb. I think I'm developing some real feelings for her. Really. I never expected to feel this way, and so soon."

"It's just," I stutter, "you couldn't have waited a little longer?"

"Waited for you?" the real estate boyfriend asks.

"You couldn't have waited just another little while?"

"Oh, we waited," says my tallest boyfriend. "We were a waiting room full of waiting for you."

"Do you even know how long you've been gone?" asks my insurance salesman, aggression teasing his voice.

"We were loyal!" yells my earnest boyfriend, whom I've never heard get mad, not once, not ever. "We only spooned each other three times, four times maybe, tops."

I picture the boyfriends supine on the living room floor, then turning on their sides in a long chain of spoon.

"And anyway," says Farren, "what do you know about loyal? You leave placements left and right. You can't hold a job to save your soul. You who botch assignments, as if there's anything more valuable in this infinite world than a day's worth of work."

"It was just that one job! Just that one time!"

"Oh please. I know about the stolen boots. About the blimp. I even know about the witch. Who do you think you're fooling, girl?"

"Farren, how could you do this to me? I don't understand."

"Is she worried about losing Farren or us?" the boyfriends cry, astonished.

"Never mind her," says my favorite boyfriend, comforting the group. "Hush, hush."

I hear them consoling one another, mending one another, on this night that was meant for celebration. Here I go, ruining everything. Here I go.

"Sometimes I have to wonder," my favorite boyfriend says, "if she even knows our names."

The line disconnects.

At the bar, I spend my earnings on a bottle of the best. "It's a bachelor party!" I tell the bartender. I toast to their engagement, their future, the boyfriends, nearly husbands, their five o'clock shadows and twelve o'clock sunburns, the spots they let me nuzzle underneath their chins. The perforation of their bitten nails, their love handles and handlebar mustaches and their muscles, their footholds for my comfort. Their inclinations and inhibitions and insecurities, lazy mornings throned in blankets, pressing against their bodies, the pillows slipping from under our heads, falling into the galactic space between wall and bed. I remember meeting them in other bars, at restaurants, on jogs and on benches. Lifting weights and running late. Happy hours and just OK hours. Attending concerts, live, unplugged. Attending parties on rooftops, attending festivals and picking fruit from trees upstate, attending other weddings. Speed dating and slow dating and dating just right, a friend of a friend of a friend. Introductions. They entered my world like a relay team, carrying and passing the baton, their racing arms spreading toward Sunday in a sweaty, sudden dash, now continuing forward, onward, and away.

I click my former employer's boots against the barstool in celebratory rhythms. If I return the boots, she'll stop trying to get in touch. I don't want her to stop trying to get in touch. I want the defiance of a life spent almost in touch. I toast to the woman who lives with her shoes. She's probably been asked to officiate the wedding.

"You're cut off, lady," the bartender says.

"Tell me about it."

I toast to Farren, to her newfound loves, to my old loves. I do love them. I do miss them. I miss them in the worst way. I miss them! I tell the bartender. My Boris, my Juan, my Hugo, my Claude, my Riko, my Roger, and Bob. To Paul H. and Paul D. and even Paul R. To Steve and Sameer and Ken, to David and Goliath, to Jack, to Jeff, to Jerry, to all of them, to all of them, to each of them alone.

"The First Temp wore a fedora," my grandmother said. "The First Temp had real style, you know. Real gumption. The First Temp packed a bag to take to the office, and her office was the entire world. She packed a bag full of mints and tissues and emergency rations, and water for drinking and a paperback for reading and a passport for easy travel. She had runs in her stockings, and she had a way to mend those runs. She could curse like a sailor, but only in front of sailors. She could run in heels! She could run everywhere. She couldn't stay anywhere.

"I knew a lot of temps in my day, back when your mother was just a little girl. I knew a woman who knew a woman whose great-cousin twice removed knew a woman who knew the First Temp. She didn't like her much. But who ever said getting liked was the point?

"The First Temp made a wish every night, and she wished for the steadiness. She wished for it to come at her fast and sudden, like a ton of bricks, like a piano from a window, falling on her head. The First Temp made a wish every night, and who am I to say if her wish came true? This isn't that kind of bedtime story, girlchick.

"The First Temp was prepared. No one is prepared

197

anymore, not these days. Remember, your grandmother tried to prepare you for something. For anything. Remember, listen to your mother. Your mother wasn't the First Temp, but she isn't the last. She knows something about something."

Home Work

Outside the bar, near the dumpster, smelling of booze and damp with rain, morning deigns to greet me. The little boy's face hovers over mine, blocking the sun like a low-flying cloud.

"Would you like to talk to me," he asks, "instead of talking to yourself?"

He can't be more than seven years old.

"Sure," I say. "Hi."

"What do you do here?" he asks.

"I look for jobs."

He doesn't laugh at me, but nods in a serious way. He offers a hand so I can sit myself upright.

"I have a temporary job for you," he says. "I'll pay you money."

I agree to follow him to his home, and to perform the job of being his mother. I throw my cigarettes in the trash, finally unlearning that old, temporary skill. He leads me down the alley and through the copse of trees, past the prison, deep into the forest, to a clearing, to a strip of stores abutting a stream. Somewhere along the way we cross the street, and I realize he's holding my hand.

There's no one else in his apartment, and the building looks all but abandoned. The sounds in the hallways have no bodies to catch them, muffle them, and they ricochet forever, lost bullets. The pitter of a mouse, the patter of shifting beams, horsehair walls wallpapered on an inconsistent slant. In one corner rests a kitchen, and in another corner a couch. A rug with one corner turned up and over, revealing hidden colonies of dust.

"Here, have a seat," he says. He points to the floor, resetting the corner of the rug with his toe. We sit across from each other.

"Where's your real mother?" I ask.

"Abducted by pirates. But she'll be home soon."

I remember Darla ripping the cap off a bottle of cider with her teeth, and I stay silent. The captives in the dungeon, the inventory in the hull.

A kitten crawls from under the couch and nestles in the boy's lap.

"Do pirates like cats?" he asks, his voice shaking.

"There's no purr in pirate," I say. "Never fear."

The cat curls against his chest and stays put when the boy stands, its claws cutting into his shirt.

"Wear this," he says to me, and he hands me her apron, her slippers, her shirtdress, her vest, her leather jacket, her Halloween costumes, her skinny jeans, her nightgown, her shower cap.

"Your real mom was pretty cool."

"Is."

We sit and do his homework on the floor until he's tired, his cheek slipping from the cup of his hand.

"Well, I'm spent," he says, and he shuffles to bed like someone older. "Make yourself at home."

The boy does exactly what he said he would, which is pay me to cook and clean and give him advice and tell him a different story every night. Sometimes I'm supposed to scold him or punish him, and sometimes I'm supposed to yell for no reason, get sad, and stare out the window.

"Like this?" I ask, leaning my forehead against the glass.

"More desperate," he says, studying my gaze. "Pick a point of focus outside and commit."

I commit to a flowerpot across the street.

"Now pick something just beyond the flowerpot, something only you can see."

I settle on a long, lithe creature of the forest, a predator from my imagination.

"Much better," he says. "You look real sad."

"Thanks," I say, smiling.

He rolls his eyes. "Stay in character!"

I cut his hair and watch him brush his teeth and lift him high so he can spit in the sink. I lift him on my shoulders and spin him around the room. I buy the groceries and cook the groceries, dividing them from their bundles and bunches and loaves, slicing and stirring and whisking, building flavor profiles, concealing vegetables, chopping at pleasing angles to create from the crusts on his plate a face with a smile. Supplying nutrients for growing boys. Tupperwared leftovers filling the fridge.

I tell him the story of how to bake a pie. I tell him the story of the daily news. I tell him the story of how he was born, which he has to tell me first.

"It was a dark and stormy night," he explains, snug under his sheets.

"Really?"

"Yes, really. Sometimes it really is."

"It was a dark and stormy night," I repeat, and he settles into my retelling.

I tell him stories about the jobs I've had, and even the boring stories make him squirm and scream. I pick the boredom until it bleeds. I don't tell him the stories are true.

"Tell me the stories, tell me the stories," he says, clapping his hands against his knees.

"OK," I say, and I take a sip of water. These are stories I know well, but sometimes a mother needs a minute. "Once upon a time, there was the assassin. There was the child."

"What else?"

"There was the house with the doors that opened and closed."

His eyes start to widen, then flutter, then droop.

"There were bombs and blimps and barnacles, and a little boy who was best of all things."

I walk out of his room backward, watching him sleep. "The box of stamps and the corkboard calendar and the pink book of message sheets to tell you what happened exactly, specifically, in detail, While You Were Out."

"Leave the light on in the hall," he calls after me, and I do.

The boy is as pale as potatoes and skinnier than the women at the agency, which is really saying something. So I perform some extra work that he wouldn't know to ask about. Like researching vitamins and malnutrition and dietary supplements. I use the money he pays me to buy medicine from the man at the bar, and my little boy's cheeks turn pink again, if they were ever pink to begin with. I remember the time I almost had an accidental little boy of my own.

"Why are you using your salary for my medicine?" He kneels in his chair so that we're the same height.

"Because I care about you, and you're sick."

"You're not supposed to care about me. That's not your responsibility."

"Actually, it is," I say.

"I promised you a job, not a family," he says, a baby snarl dilapidating the base of his chin. He's already growing up cruel, I think, brokenhearted, primed to break hearts. I wonder if he'll grow up to be someone's boyfriend, their only boyfriend, or one of many. Someone's father. Father of many. Someone's pal. Someone else's kid. Then I remember his mother, the pirates, Darla. I crush the vitamins and hide them in his food.

"I thought I made myself clear," he says later, spooning the evidence onto a saucer. Mashed squash pebbled with pills.

"You're right," I say. "I'm sorry," and finally he smiles. He dangles a string for his cat to catch, and the cat is pleased to catch it.

The boy tells me about his ten-year plan, about how he wants to run a business when he grows up, how he could run a business very fairly. A business he could pass on to his kids, something that would stick. "First you need a prospectus, like this," he says, drawing a circle with his finger on the kitchen counter. "Then you start hiring," he adds, "like how I hired you."

"You hired me next to a dumpster," I say.

"You've got to start somewhere."

The boy's plan sounds bright and metallic, so sleek that it hurts to look in the direction of his dreams.

"In that case, can I have a job at your company?" I ask.

"Of course," he says, "pending approval of your application."

We go to the store and pick out the right kind of pens for his company, the kind a real businessman might use. We click them open and test them on papers filled with scratch. He carries them home, bag swinging around his wrist. Then he lines them up on the desk next to his bed. We do homework and dot the i's and cross the t's like honest professionals.

I notice that when I say certain unfamiliar words, he repeats them later in conversation, mispronouncing them, which makes my heart feel larger than ever before. He grows and grows and grows.

When he finds out about the Chairman, he thinks I have a superpower. "Can I see him? Can you tell him to appear?" he marvels.

"Oh, he comes and goes as he pleases."

"But who tells him to go away?"

"No one. He never goes away."

He pretends to talk with the Chairman in his room, down the hall, and into the kitchen. I can hear him exclaiming and reasoning, discussing everything from math homework to pets.

"Whoa," he says, collapsing on the ground. "Whoa, the Chairman is so cool!"

"Whoa!" I say.

"Did you see him? He was hanging out with me!"

"I totally saw."

"Whoa."

When I'm up late, walking about in his mother's slippers, my necklace starts to burn, and the Chairman keeps me company watching late night television talk shows.

"Did I miss him again?" the boy asks in the morning.

"Your sweater is too small," I say, and we go shopping for a new one, with a zipper and patches and pockets to hold the treasures that come with being a kid. Then he's too big for the new sweater, and we shop for a newer one. His parade of sweaters could stretch around the apartment and over the cat and under the rug.

I sign permission slips, practicing the forgery for field trips and class projects. Yes, my boy can travel to the clock tower.

Yes, my boy can dissect a frog. And also, yes, he may. After school, he runs down to the stream with other boys his age. One of them wears a helmet, because he has a new bike. They share the bike and throw away the helmet. They take turns. They all pile on at once, like bees on a hive, and the bike falls flat on its side.

I save my money and I buy him a bike of his own.

"You really need to stop doing this," he says, shaking his head, disappointed that I still don't seem to understand.

I shrug. "I can't help it."

"Try," he says, grabbing the bicycle handles, the bright red bell above the brake. His face changes for a minute, softens. "I'll keep it," he says, "but only to make you happy."

"Fine," I say, and I smile to myself for weeks.

"Don't mention it," he says, and he rides his bike into the sunset like the cowboy I've raised him to be.

The other mothers gather at a picnic table for coffee, and I join them.

"Whose mom are you again?" one of them asks. She has a short blond bob that leaves her neck long and free.

I point to the boy who is mine.

"Did you get your nose done?" they ask. "Did you gain some weight?" "Did you dye your hair?" Not remembering but somewhere deep down suspecting, suggesting, I'm not the person I pretend to be.

"Yes," I say, to all their questions. "All those things, yes."

"That explains it!" says the blond bob. She offers me a cracker and some cheese. She offers me a glass of wine, later, on her couch.

"The kids!" they exclaim, and they talk about their kids.

"The pets!" they exclaim, and they talk about their pets.

"The husbands!" they exclaim, and they talk about their husbands.

The plurality of their lives, I think, trying to cast a line to a person, place, or thing I can claim for myself.

"What about you?" asks a mother with adult braces.

"What about me?" I ask, genuinely wanting an answer. No one answers. We read magazines and the glass of wine in my hand refills itself thanks to the magical properties of women gathered in a room.

We volunteer to chaperone a school dance. The boys stand around a box of donuts, watching its contents with the intensity of attempted levitation. We stand near the door, guarding the comings and goings of our children, our cheeks flushed with the cold.

"Why not a slow dance?" says the blond bob, and she changes the music. Now the boy and his friends are holding the donut box, all hands on deck, as if to say, We're clearly busy with something else right now.

The girls coagulate in the darkest corner of the room.

"I love this song," says the blond bob. She dances with another mom.

I look down and my boy is standing by my side. He touches my wrist.

"These pants are all wrong," he says.

"What's wrong with them?"

"Everything," he says, almost crying.

I walk back to our apartment and retrieve a pair of khakis. I walk back in the dark, khakis slung over my shoulder like a pelt for his survival.

"Thanks," he says, running off to change in the bathroom. He tucks his wrong jeans in my bag and returns to his friends, to their deliberations over donuts.

"Wasn't that fun?" I ask him on our way home at the end of the night.

"It was a kind of fun," he says.

We walk the rest of the way in silence. When we get home, he suggests I get mad, then get sad, then stare out the window. "That's how it should be," he explains, walking off to bed.

The moms sit at the picnic table with their coffees. We talk about the boys. We talk about the bombs. We talk about the petition for the thing no one remembers. We bake cookies and bring them to bake sales and sell the cookies for more than they're worth.

"I feel so undervalued," says the blond bob. We go for walks sometimes in the afternoon. She starts to sob. "Do you value me?" she asks.

"Of course," I say, patting her round, bright skull. Like polishing a prize.

We walk to the stream and take our shoes off and put our feet in the water. It feels cool and fresh between our toes, and then it feels like nothing. We wade until we're numb, continents of snow drifting over the tops of our feet.

"And at what cost," she asks, a question in a conversation we've never had.

My boy leaves his keys in the door and gives me a fright. Is he old enough to drive? I can't remember.

He and his friends go on a field trip and learn how to craft artisan paninis. They come over and demonstrate their new skill. They make one just for me, with thick bread and the nicest cheese you can buy at the store, with aioli and fresh tomatoes and ribbons of basil, and it's simply the very best thing I've ever tasted.

"It's the very best thing I've ever tasted," I tell them.

"Hooray!"

"In my whole life."

I scoop shiny spheres of ice cream for them, and they play board games on the floor, falling asleep with a milky lacquer over their lips. The old cat traipses through the casualties, knocking over piles of cards, swatting at the plastic pieces.

I stand to watch the scene, the boy and his friends scattered on the rug, heads almost touching, limbs landing this way and that. Tomorrow, I think, I'll rent movies. They can watch movies all day long. They can just sit here and watch as many movies as they want. How many days are like that? It's a good kind of day to have. I make a shopping list for all the different kinds of days I want to provide for my son, and I cross this day off the list.

The moon lights up the living room like a screen. I go to my room to get some sleep.

In the morning, I wake up already standing. I'm standing over the kitchen counter. The boy is standing across from me. When did he get so tall? Do I see the beginnings of a beard?

"You were sleepwalking," he says. His friends stand behind him, providing some unclarified moral support.

"Where did I go this time?" I laugh.

"You went to collect your things," he says, opening one hand and revealing my eye patch. "Pirates," he murmurs to his friends, barely holding his voice in place.

"It's not what you think. It's a costume," I explain, "for Halloween," my heart already breaking. I try to lie every day, practicing mostly on myself.

"Is this a costume too?" he asks. In his other hand, he reveals the brooch in the shape of a nautilus shell. The same shape found in the nerves collecting behind his eye at this very moment. In his eye he collects a tear, then another. "This was my mother's," he says. "Why do you have it?"

"I don't remember," I say. I muster all my human resources to not collapse, to not die right here on the spot.

"Get out."

"No," I say.

His friends look at me, unfriendly friends. The old cat hisses.

"*Out*," he says, pointing to the door.

"I'm sorry, but I can't just leave you here alone." I place my hands flat on the kitchen counter, which I have come to think of as my kitchen counter. My kitchen. My cat. My home. My child. "You're just a child," I say.

The light sort of shifts. Does he have a tattoo? A mustache?

"I'll call the police," he says, and I know he means it. I know I won't be as lucky a second time around, running from the law. "This transaction," he says, "is not open to your interpretation."

As I exit the apartment, I'm scolding him, punishing him, yelling for no reason, getting sad, and walking out the door. I thought my steadiness had nearly arrived, but here I am, alone again.

"Don't come back, ever," say his friends.

There are lots of different kinds of mothers. He never specified which kind he wanted.

This is me, the type of mother who leaves.

"Where you heading?" the blond bob yells in my direction. She's standing at the corner.

I don't respond.

"Hey! Where you going?"

I keep walking.

The artisan panini shop has been replaced by a bank. All the same bank. New stores. All the same stores. I don't recognize a single thing, and I recognize everything. It's exhausting. Once my heels were solid, but now they're rotted through, the infrastructure of the stolen boots laid bare. I once walked along and sometimes skipped. Now I skip minutes, seconds, hours.

I find a job flipping burgers, and that's all there is to that. I keep expecting the job to reveal itself in full, but not all jobs are icebergs, with hidden miles of work. Some jobs are just jobs. I tuck my hair into a net and conduct daily dealings with grease and fire. I catch my reflection in the sneeze guard, and she's a stranger.

At the new bank, they're hiring human metal detectors. I drink a thick milkshake filled with special particles, and now, when someone walks past me, I can detect their metal. I can also detect their mettle, an unintended side effect.

You explain to your supervisor that you can detect their despair, and your supervisor declares that this makes sense. "Despair clings to the metal you're already detecting."

We detectors have the simplest of intentions: to keep people out, to keep people in. To sense something extra, a sheath or a shroud, a holiday bonus, an elbowed bracket that extends past the boundaries of the body. The boundaries of the bank are high and tinseled with security cameras, electrified with wire, gilded with lights that lead me back to my place at the front entrance.

I detect some metal in the shape of a toy.

I detect some metal in the shape of a nautilus shell.

I detect some metal in the shape of a knife and look up. Laurette's face looks back. The sorrow I detect is so deep and unbearable, I throw up. Seasickness, sorrowsickness.

When I collect myself, Laurette has disappeared, and my supervisor stands over my head.

"Pack your things, obviously."

Then it's unemployment for months, for maybe one hundred years. Unemployment: Don't say that word in front of the baby, my mother had scolded her mother. Such shame, the first time I have ever been without occupation. But time seeps in around shame's edges. Unaccounted time, time without sheets or stamps or cards. Time introduces herself to me, to each of my empty hours. Time is a new acquaintance, and she does something funny to my limbs, my worries, my anger, my life. Garbage sidles up against the curb, like a lonely lover looking for affection. There is no one living in that building across the way. A tree lost half its branches yesterday, and everyone continues to walk through the ghost of its shade. Unaccounted time has its own inventory.

On a cold morning, I feel a lump in my throat that lasts all day.

On a humid afternoon, I find a stray pamphlet tucked inside my boot, stinging the bottom of my foot for who knows how long. I hold the pamphlet to my chest until it burns like a rash. I make a wish on the pamphlet to go home. For a place to belong. I even click my broken heels together.

On a rainy evening, I wait at the dock, in the harbor, near the public beach.

On a foggy night, in the distance, a billowing sail, the silhouette of a vessel on the move. I run with everything I own, which is nothing, just my necklace, hot as fire, just me and the Chairman of the Board, racing to meet the pirates at the shore.

The gods created the First Temporary so they could take a break. "Let there be some spare time," they said, "and cover for us, won't you? Here are all our passwords and credentials." She fell from the husk of a meteor and glowed with no particular ambition. They had to pin her down so she would not float away, so very much distracted was this new kind of soul, so subject to drift. The gods had not yet created gravity. This was back when toads without occupation soared straight up to the clouds, back when employment was the only kind of honest weight you could apply to a life.

The First Temporary was encouraged to replicate the gods' image, even though she was not specifically created to resemble any of them. This was a job description added ex post facto. And so she forever was to learn her permutations, her shorthand methods of duplication, contortions of empathy. Her handwriting was the perfect facsimile of the handwriting everyone expected. She lived in the space between who she was and whom she was meant to replace. More responsibilities for the First Temporary, and she completed the tasks with aplomb, filed the backup documents, checked each item off her list.

"Burn this bush," one god said, and so she did.

"Now put the bush back the way it was," another god said, and the First Temp learned the drudgery of tasks done and undone, the brutal makings and unmakings of the earth.

"Can I stay? Permanently?" she asked, and the gods just laughed and went to lunch.

The First Temporary studied the world. She noted the shortcomings of the gods, their tempers and their feuds. It was their bureaucracy that allowed for her existence. She noted the fallacy of permanence in a world where everything ends and desired that kind of permanence all the same.

One afternoon, when her work was finished, she had an hour to spare for insubordination. With her eyes closed, she created a series of friends. No, employees. No, colleagues, she thought. The temporaries emerged from the soles of her sensible shoes, then scattered with the wind. She reached down from the sky to find them, dipped her hand into a stream and pulled them from the current like an oar from a canoe, digging deep into the water and lifting forth. She wiped them off and patted them dry and gave them leather planners, inky pens, laminated instructions for how to interact with the world.

They were travelers, created as such with the breeze at their backs, meant to fill any gaps the gods had forgotten. There were stars in the sky but still no moon, and a temp-orary rounded her body into an iridescent orb. *"Great idea,"* one god said, feasting on honeydew, and the moon was made in her image. The intentions of the moose were always unclear to the elk, and a temporary vaulted her arms into antlers so the animals could lock themselves into thorny disagreements, then eventually, solutions. Shoelaces were always frayed at the ends. A temporary reduced herself to a fraction of her size, capped an aglet on the laces with her new, plastic countenance. The sky would not meet the sea, and so a temporary folded herself into a thin connecting strip of mist and air, henceforth called a horizon.

The world accumulated more stuff but stayed the same size. Clutter gave the impression of completion, but the First Temp knew there was still work to be done. "Get clever," she told her colleagues. They noticed the absence of microwave-safe pottery and hollowed their bodies into bowls, plates, mugs, forgotten, and left to sit in their own filth. They noticed the absence of storage and stretched themselves into closets. They noticed the continuous departures of kindness and sloughed their skins to wear their hearts on their sleeves as reminders. They always noticed, with relief, prodigal kind-ness making its inevitable return.

The temporaries grew sturdier legs, more robust arms, less prone to willy-nilly transformation. They evolved and took their places in the crowd. They fit in and filled in. Thou-sands of years changed over like a crossing signal, and the temporaries crossed the street. Sometimes the crosswalk was not enough for traffic, and yet, a temporary hit by a bus was rarely mourned or replaced. After all, who would bother replacing a replacement? In this way, the temporaries had a sort of elastic permanence of their own.

"But now will you hire me full-time?" asked the First Temp.

"Come into our office," the gods said, and she followed them to their desks.

"I really love your creativity," one god said with a hint of ellipsis, and the First Temp correctly predicted a forthcoming, ominous but.

There were no full-time positions open.

"Will there be an opening sometime soon?"

"Perhaps," the gods said. "Soon is relative in the grand scheme of our enterprise."

"Will there be an opening sometime soon?" the First Temp asked after another hundred years.

"Soon is relative."

"Soon?" She asked, when her calendar reminded her to check again.

"Soon is relative."

"Soon?"

"Soon."

The First Temp rolled herself out of the gods' office and into the bathroom at the end of the hall. It wasn't really a hall-way, you'll understand, but more the approximation of those emotions associated with walking and arriving. It wasn't really a bathroom, either, but it felt the way office bathrooms do. Fluorescent, echoing, cold and tiled.

The First Temp locked herself in a bathroom stall and became the First Temp to Cry in the Bathroom at Work, the very first of her kind. The hot tears fell down her face, and she used her sleeves to blot them away. She sat on the toilet seat in her dress, tapping her foot, waiting for the moment to subside. She was undone, and that's when a handful of tissues appeared under the door.

The First Temp emerged and found herself surrounded by her temporary colleagues. They held mugs of tea and tubes of mascara and pouches of chocolates. "It's OK!" they said, patting her shoulders and fixing her hair. "We'll wait until you're feeling better. We've got nothing else to do. We have nowhere else to be, only here with you."

After she had collected herself, she returned to her desk with an escort of temporaries. Then they dispersed again, through the office, out into the world.

"We're so sorry!" said the gods, hovering over the First Temp's desk. She felt their sorrow was genuine. She knew when they were genuine because she was built to feel the world through active, staggered checks of compassion. She could not help but understand where they were coming from, because it was where she came from, too, because she was meant to begin where other people ended. She lived in the acute angle that forecasted the world's limitations. If they had locked her in a room made of ice, she would have probably seen their side of things, shimmering in her own reflection.

She filled in when the gods went for long weekends. She filled her days until none were left, and then she started over. She watched her colleagues while they slept, and prayed for them to find their steadiness, even if she could not. The lunch breaks were short and staggered. There was always a small sandwich in a small sandwich bag. There was always a deadline or a timeline. There was always a brightly colored *pen and a fresh notebook. She could find glimmers of joy in this ephemeral life.*

She guided the temporaries through their placements, preserved their infinite time in this infinite world. To perhaps ensure for them something more sacred than survival.

Post Work

I'm drinking ale with Darla on the hundredth voyage of her unmarked vessel.

"We never got around to picking out that logo," she says, her mermaid hair swept into a messy bun.

The ship makes a swipe across the sea, rocking through rickety waves. A series of storms has wrecked the crew, and many faces are missing from the crowd.

"Like bombs falling from the sky," Darla says, trying to describe the blasts that sent waves up and over the sails. You nod at the simile, which is perhaps closer to the truth than Darla can imagine. "And then, all the prisoners, released. Not to mention that dragon. Is it a dragon or something worse?"

The pirate captain's wife sits alone at the mast of the ship, watching an old movie projected on the sails.

"It's been a rough time."

"Pearl?" I ask.

Darla shakes her head.

Two Pearls lost, none remain. When everyone is gone, it doesn't matter who came first, who was original, who was not.

My first instinct: secure myself to the prow in protest of my grief. My second instinct: race to the dungeon, find the boy's missing mother. But no, there are new captives here, new people, new problems, the old captives gone long ago. It's been ages. There's a crease that runs along my brow, and I'm not sure where it's from. Darla serves me a plate of grub and forces it down my throat. Maurice flies overhead, the real Maurice, squawking at the fading sunlight.

"How are your grandparents, the ones who live in Florida?" I ask Darla.

"Dead."

Safe at my old porthole, I spot a human barnacle riding the back of a whale. A special kind of breed. I wonder where it goes. Where I will go next, what I will do, what kind of adhesive I am made of, if any kind at all. I think I finally know something, but the knowledge slips away. And then the sea mist and the clouds and the fog return, the trusty dispersion and reconstitution of water.

I tie the knots required of me and file the daily logs. I drink coffee with the executive assistant, sitting on the plank with our legs dangling free. It's like nothing happened, like nothing changed, like I've been sitting here all along, right where I started. My world, done and undone.

"Never would Darla do to others as they would do to her," I say.

"I do them one better," Darla says, and we laugh like crazy. Or no, not like crazy. Just like friends. When I'm in a rush to file the daily logs, Darla cleans my bunk for me, makes my bed, organizes my cabin. I do the same for her. We do this thing for each other. We make gestures at the world that ricochet toward an intended person. I thought I understood Darla.

I thought I had practiced the kind of empathy that would allow me to replace her. But there are new pieces of information every day. She does this thing with her ears when she thinks no one is looking. She wiggles them. How long does it take to accurately replace a person, I wonder? Certainly longer than a life. An eye patch doesn't replace the eye, it just provides temporary coverage.

"To Pearl," she says.

"To Pearls," I say.

Sitting in the middle of the sea, we eat under the stars, the sky reflected in the water, an infinite display of light.

Darla invites me to serve as the new first mate of human resources.

"Permanently?"

"Sure," Darla says, thumbs in her pockets. "We have so many people to replace."

It would be easy. How long have I been here, anyway? I consider the roughness of my hands, the soreness in my throat. "I'll think about it," I say, but I've already thought about it. It's the only thing I think about, the ways in which I can't stay. I close my eyes and wait for the steadiness to arrive, but it never does.

On a beautiful afternoon in spring, when the air hits my skin at just the right temperature, with just the right distribution of breeze and sun, the port accepts our ship with a quake. I jolt awake from where I nap in the crow's nest and find myself positioned at eye level with the sign that hangs over this part of the harbor, a billboard of sorts, a beacon painted in large block letters, stomping across the sky.

"Our parent company," says Darla.

Something familiar after so much time away.

Major Corp.

I can't go to my old apartment, my apartment no longer mine. So I walk across town to the Major Corp offices. Major proportions, minor distinctions. The building seems to acquiesce to my visit. The lobby soothes me in a way I can't describe. I don't have a keycard to swipe, but I'm allowed to enter all the same, just as I expected.

"We've been waiting for you," a woman says, holding the door for me. She looks like the woman I fired all those years ago.

"Are you the woman I fired all those years ago?" I ask.

She laughs and smiles, then holds an outstretched arm to the elevators. Those fabulous, fabulous arms.

It's something that Darla said, sticking in my throat, that brings me to this place. I clutch my necklace and make my way through the halls, past the snack pantry, the cubicles, the corner office. And there, just as I remembered, the boardroom. The portrait of the Chairman. The long, shiny board table. The coffee service in the corner. The high-backed leather chairs.

My necklace burns. "What are you waiting for?" the Chairman asks, standing near the windows, the skyline as a backdrop. His voice goes straight from the necklace to my head, and I follow his instructions.

I stand on the table, and it is just high enough that I can touch my fingers to the boardroom ceiling. With a long stretch of pinky, I poke it gently, then harder, then with a punch, it rises. A small square of plaster pops free, a bracket, a tomb. I use my arms to lift myself up and up and into the sky.

For it is here, in this extra room above the highest floor, where I find my inheritance: boxes of company documents, Major Corp suddenly mine. A long letter from the Chairman of the Board explaining how to run a business, how to run a business very fairly. Here are my passwords and credentials. Here are my favorite foods. Here is a list of acceptable office attire. Here is what you do when someone undermines your authority. Here is the key to the office, and here is the key to a secret office. Here, all for you.

And I've been with you the whole time, he says, in his beautiful penmanship. There he was, in my apartment. There he was, in the box in the back of my closet. There he was, on a pirate ship and in a murder shack and the vault deep within the bank. There he was in the blimp, in the tunnels, when I tried to be a mother. In the hospital, the man as tall as a crane, hovering over my own mother, covering her hand like a tarp for the tubes and needles. Making her laugh. Her tallest, favorite boyfriend. No judgment, just here, just there, not for your survival. For support. A man about town, to look after me. There, in the dust on the chain I wear above my heart like a duty.

Parent company, Darla had said.

My father.

I climb back down into the boardroom, but he's gone. I try to summon him through my necklace, but no, he's not a genie. My necklace runs cold now, and always.

That lump in the back of my throat again. I try to swallow it, but the feeling stays.

Exit Interview

Can you tell us more about this lump in your throat, in relation to your job performance?

The lump grew larger during my years here at Major Corp. It was a good lump, like a weight applied to my life. Like an emotion always reinforcing my decisions. I learned how to run a business, and I ran it very fairly. On Mondays and Fridays, I interviewed potential hires. I hired Darla full-time, and she set aside her life at sea. I hired some of the boyfriends. I finally saw them again.

How would you describe your reunion with your boyfriends?

"You!" we said, and we ran toward each other. We embraced. It wasn't the hug I expected. It was a nesting doll of affection, an act of warmth that contained all previously lost warmth.

Did this present any unexpected challenges?

"How's Farren?" I asked them. "Oh, you know," they said. They weren't my boyfriends anymore, but we were friends all the same. "You're one of us," they said. They left their mugs in their cubicles, scrubbed and buffed and always clean. "Good morning," they said when they walked past my open office door.

"Good morning," I responded, kicking my feet up on my desk. Our reconciliation only augmented the lump in my throat.

What would your mother say?
Something about being sensible, something about an honest day's work. Something about the size of my office.

Can you name a specific challenge you had to tackle?
Under my supervision, we wrestled the Director of Pamphlets back into her cave. It took seven pirate ships and three boyfriends. They guarded her cave until she returned to her human form. "I know it'll probably kill me," she said, "staying here all alone." "This will kill her," a doctor said, and then it did. The doctor knew what he was talking about. At Major Corp, we give great benefits, and of course, the Director of Pamphlets was an employee of one of our subsidiaries. I thought, When I die, it will be like leaving a job without time to clear my desk.

Can you name a specific instance where you felt unqualified for your position?
I've never felt qualified for anything other than lacking qualifications. When I water my plant, I feel especially unqualified, because she's always on the brink of death.

Were you able to achieve the steadiness?
One afternoon, the lump in my throat went down. As in, I swallowed it. It felt like a glowing rock moving through my body, past my heart, down into my core. I was sitting at

my desk, doing nothing. It was just like Anna said. I'd given up, so steadiness was given to me. When I wasn't looking. For a while, I was so happy I could've burst like a dirigible. For a while.

And how did you handle the setbacks?
To be honest, I didn't notice at first. Everyone was growing old. Everyone was dying. When everyone was dead, I was still alive. And then the thought settled like a new lump, this time on the back of my head. I held my head and it started to hurt. I'd always thought permanence meant I would be like everyone else. What it meant was something else entirely. What it meant was *permanence*. Actual forever permanence. I would get sick and instantly get well. I would cut my finger and watch the skin seal itself shut.

In your leather-bound planner, you frequently refer to feeling like a fossil. Can you elaborate?
I mean to say that I'm a literal fossil. I'm a rock formation, holding many impressions from many objects, many beings, many times. I am a walking remembrance. When the city streets finally filled with water, when the water continued to rise, I would sometimes take a canoe out through the opening in the upper parking garage. I would go looking for Anna, for other permanents like me. What I found wasn't Anna, not anyone at all. And then, back up to the top of the Major Corp tower, the only part of the city unsubmerged. Amazing how the sun continues to set, how I remain.

Are you also writing the questions in this exit interview?
Yes.

Did you feel adequately equipped to deal with death?
It didn't get easier, but with time, I was able to hold more death inside me. When my favorite boyfriend died, I was only as deep as a closet. There was no room to contain my grief. When cows went extinct, I was perhaps as deep as a basement. When the human race disappeared, I was as deep as the sea.

The Last Temporary lived on the top floor of the highest sky-scraper in an empty, flooded city. Every morning, she rowed her canoe down Canal Street, now an actual canal, gliding past the avenues, no rush hour to speak of, no traffic jams anymore. Above and around the carcasses of real estate, she searched for proof of life.

The Last Temporary was not a temporary at all. She was permanently here, a permanent, keeping watch, filling in for all that was gone. The gods had long abandoned things, but the Last Temp remained, the remains of the world, the remainder of a job unfinished. Whether or not the job of humanity was completed adequately was not for her to say. She witnessed the brutal unmaking of the earth, the tasks unspooled, the people undone, the mazes unwound, the houses unfolded, laid flat like paper swans, the knots at the bottom of the ocean, unraveled into long skeins of rope, thin straight lines trailing for fathoms where once there had lived tangled signs of existence.

"It's always possible that I will ferry someone to shore," the Last Temp thought, "someone like me."

She summoned the strength of the very First Temp, of her mother, of her grandmother, too, all the people now departed.

When she closed her eyes, she could muster the force to fill in for every single person, and for their favorite people, and for their enemies, and for their boyfriends, and for their children, and for their employers, their wives, their wardens, their supervisors, their supervisees, their acquaintances, fugitives, fathers, fiancés, friends, even me, even you. She could steal everyone's shoes, never return them, wear them forever.

On the roof of the skyscraper, listening to the breeze between their bodies: the Last Temp and every single person who had ever lived. The infinite world on its axis, the axis of her spine pointed toward theirs, and theirs, and theirs. To hold the entire history of everything. Something more sacred than just survival. "It's the least I can do," she thinks, "While You Are Out."

Acknowledgments

For the work of fearless navigation and dedication, thank you to my brilliant agent, Monika Woods. To Ruth Curry and Emily Gould for the work of mending words and cracking open sentences. I am so grateful to you, guardians of this book's nouns and verbs and strange little spirit.

Thank you to the effervescent team at Coffee House Press. To Anitra Budd, Nica Carrillo, Lizzie Davis, Annemarie Eayrs, Daley Farr, Laurie Herrmann, and Carla Valadez, thank you for your guidance and enthusiasm, for the work of building a beautiful paper home where my novel can live.

For the work of encouragement, thank you to my mentors and professors, especially Ben Marcus, Sam Lipsyte, Diane Williams, and Timothy Donnelly. To Daniel Menaker, for equal parts advice, wisdom, and kibitzing.

Thank you to Mary and Hank, wherever you are, my very first employers in New York. Thank you to Alec Guettel for (still) being the coolest boss. It's nice work if you can get it.

For the business of shelter, inspiration, solitude, camaraderie, and financial support, I am grateful to Columbia University, Haverford College, the Edward F. Albee Foundation, the Table 4 Writers Foundation, the Folger Shakespeare Library, and the New York Foundation for the Arts. And thank you to *n+1* for giving the short-story version of *Temporary* its original home.

For the labor of reading my many drafts, of hand-holding and dog-earing, of tempering work with play, I am devoted to and filled with admiration for my dear colleagues and friends: Dennis Norris II, Xuan Juliana Wang, Ruchika Tomar, Diane Cook, Mary South, Rebekah Bergman, Aaron Allen, Jessamine Chan, Emma Copley Eisenberg, Brendan Embser, Liana Finck, Sasha Fletcher, Rosie Guerin, Anna Krieger, Ethan Hartman, Adam Levy, Ashley Nelson Levy, Monica Lewis, Mandy Medley, Steve and Emma Nelson, Elizabeth Reinhard, Wendy Salinger, and Sara Sligar.

To Caitlin, Megan, Sarah, and Katie for their very untemporary friendships. I am so grateful to have you in my life. Thank you to my family of Leichters, Griffins, and Bertwells, for accepting and believing in me. And thank you to my mom, the hardest working person I know.

This book is for the plants that work to make the air breathable, for the tide that works to make the waves survivable. For our planet, who works for us even when we haven't worked for her.

Most of all, Matt, this book exists for and because of you. For heart-work, soul-work, the work of building and sharing a life. We two might be workaholics, but loving you requires no work at all.